THIN FIRE

BY NANCI LITTLE

Madwoman Press, Inc.
1993

This is a work of fiction. Any resemblance between characters in this book and actual persons, living or dead, is coincidental.

Cover by Bonnie Liss and Pat Tong of Phoenix Graphics, Winter Haven, Florida

Edited by Diane Benison and Catherine S. Stamps

Printed in the United States on acid-free paper

Library of Congress Cataloging-in-Publication Data

Little, Nanci, 1955–
    Thin fire / by Nanci Little.
        p. cm.
    ISBN 0-9630822-4-8 (soft cover :   acid free paper) :
    1. Lesbians—United States—Fiction. 2. United States—Armed forces—Gays—Fiction. I. Title.
    PS3562.I78295T48   1993
    813'.54—dc20

                                              93-6312
                                              CIP

To Sue,
who understands the goddess
of that other planet
. . .
and to my family
whom I can only
deeply thank.

In Memory
H.S.M.

BOOK ONE: NIKKI

CHAPTER ONE

So this was the sickin aydee reppledepple. She hadn't known what to expect. There was precious little information available from the bawling sergeants at the Initial In-Processing Center; they were, in their words, up to their asses in alligators and didn't have time for questions from trainees just in from Fort Jackson or Fort Dix or Fort Anyfuckingwhere.

"Ya goan t'th' reppledepple," they barked, when asked for information of destiny. "Now siddown, I'm upta my ass in alligators here." And when one of them roared, "everybody goan t'th' sickin aydee reppledepple over here!" Nikki Cole went over there because over there seemed to be her only option. For the ten thousandth time, she wondered why she'd joined the Army. She hauled a duffle bag jammed with seventy-five pounds of basic issue and a suitcase with civvies and personal gear onto the bus before one of those alligator-chewed sergeants took a mind to help her up the steps via a slap on the ass. It occurred to her that ditching the duffle, missing the bus and finding a chance to slip away with the suitcase had been a brief option.

Too late now; she got on the bus. *Sickin aydee reppledepple, whatever you are, here I come.*

"2d Armored Division Replacement Detachment," said the sign in front of a ramblingly dilapidated old building that had been built for temporary barracks during WWII and was, in 1976, still in use because it was standing, though its duration in that upright condition was in serious question. *I suppose I could have expected reppledepple out of Replacement Detachment*, she thought, *after four ubiquitously acronymic months.*

"Giddawffada bus, ya fuggin trainees," a sergeant bawled, and the riders simmered in resentment; Advanced Individual Training drill sergeants had promised they'd never hear that disparagement again. "You're not trainees anymore," they'd said with reluctant pride. "You passed the toughest tests of a peacetime Army: Basic and Advanced Individual Training. You were good trainees. Go out and be good soldiers."

Ayuh. Right.

If In-Processing had been a loony bin, this was chaos. The old bawling NCOs were replaced with new ones, not quite so abrasive but not from any friendly planet, either. The replacements (why aren't we called repples now, she wondered, instead of trainees) made a hasty formation, five ranks of ten.

"Adams!"

"Here, drill sergeant!"

"Do I look like a fuckin drill sergeant? Does this look like fuckin basic trainin? You're in the fuckin reglar Army now, at Fort Hood Texas homa Patton's own sickin armored vision say here! Adams!"

"Here."

"Andrews!"

"Here."

"Azimus!"

"Yo."

"Did I say say yo? Did you douchebags hear me say you should say yo? Are you a fuckin Marine or just a stupid muhfucka? Same thing. Yo; Jesus Christ. Azimus!"

"Here."

"Cole!"

"Here." It came out he-ah; Boston did what Boston did with words like that.

"He-yah," the sergeant muttered. "Fuckin Yankee."

"Ayuh, we won," she muttered back, and the guy beside her tittered. Both of them donated fifty pushups to the sergeant's hope chest. She snapped hers out smartly; getting dropped for a lip-infraction fifty had been routine for her at Forts McClellan and Dix, and she still hadn't learned to keep her mouth shut—or, she refused to be silenced. Just a matter of perspective.

The sergeant finished his roll and they made a line. It was ninety degrees on the seventh of April. They talked and smoked, made quiet rude remarks about the sergeants, about Fort Hood, about the division. The line crawled forward. Cole gave up her paperwork to the sergeant who had made her do the pushups. He grinned at her. She stared back impassively. "Yeah, you'll learn," he grinned. "You a homo, or lookin for an officer to marry?" She took a notebook from her sleeve pocket and wrote his comment with his name and rank down in it, checked her watch, added the time and date. He finished her processing without affording further reason to preserve his words for posterity or forwarding to the Inspector General.

"Thank you, Sergeant Gaither," she said sweetly, when he handed back her papers. He glowered. She gave him an innocent smile and moved along. Until a truck came from her new unit—the five-oh-deuce; nothing got called what it looked like on paper, it seemed—her time was her own. She

found space on a bench in the dayroom and gratefully, she
sat.
    "Man oh," said a lanky blond man next to her. "What a
drill. If I knew what half them damn letters mean, it'd be one
thing. Why don't they just say it instead of spell it? What do
they call that, when they do that?"
    "Alphabet soup mostly. Sometimes they're real acro-
nyms." She found a cigarette in her pocket; he lit it for her.
"My favorite one is FTA," she said, and he grinned; FTA meant
fuck the army, and it was usually the first acronym a recruit
learned.
    "I'm Lowell Bates." He offered a hand. "Ardmore,
Oklahoma."
    "Nikki Cole." She shook his hand. "Boston."
    "So what's your assignment?" She told him the unit.
"Oh. I'm signal. I's hopin' we might be in the same unit. I'd
like to take you out. You're cute."
    "Spare me, guy," she said wearily. "I didn't join the
Army to ball my way through it, contrary to what seems to
be popular opinion about why women join."
    "Yeah? So eat shit, y'uppity Yankee cunt," he snarled,
and left; she didn't miss him.
    There was a pool table in the middle of the room; a tall
female soldier with heavy-lidded hazel eyes was chalking a
cue that surely hadn't come off the dayroom wall, with its
satin-wrapped handle and silver weights; "Eight in the side,
off the rail." She leaned across the table for a smooth stroke;
the cue ball cushioned off and kissed the eight to drop it into
the side pocket. "Oh fuck me," said a lanky black private, and
he slapped a ten-spot into her hand and racked his cue in
disgust.
    Nikki watched as the tall woman took on all comers at
ten dollars a game, draping her graceful height and reach

across the table, her slim hands stroking nine men away from their money before a willowy, thin-mustached black man whose name tag identified him as Davis won the break and ran them as he called them to accept ten from her. "Nice stickage," she said, and took her cue with her as she threaded through the crowd, a pack of Kools in hand. Nikki relinquished her spot on the bench and followed.

She found her leaning against the peeling-painted wall of the building, a cigarette dangling from her lip and the cue under her arm as she tucked her winnings into a wallet and the wallet into a hip pocket. "Excuse me," Nikki said, and the tall woman looked up. "Are you gay?"

A small smile twitched to the tall woman's mouth, almost reaching her large and expressive hazel eyes. "No. No, I'm not."

"Oh." *I would have sworn.* "Okay. Just wondered."

"You're brave, asking that of someone with a big stick in her hand."

Nikki shrugged. "Didn't hurt either one of us for me to ask." She went back into the dayroom. Davis still had control of the table, and from the way he shot, it looked as if he'd have it for a while. Her place on the bench had been taken; she leaned against the wall and watched the pool players. No women challenged Davis; of the dozen enlisted women in the room, none looked anything but straight. Nikki Cole sighed, and smoked, and watched the games. The noise was incredible, the babble of fifty different conversations underscored by thumping disco music and the rattle and click of pool balls. She had a nasty headache lurking around the back of her neck. She went outside again, trying to escape the noise, and found the shady side of the building. The tall woman with the pool cue was there, smoking, leaning against the wall, talking with a brawnily handsome man about fishing. Nikki shook her head, keeping a distance respectful of their privacy. *In a pig's ass you're not*, she thought. *Maybe you don't know it yet, but honey, you're as lesbian as I am.*

❏   ❏   ❏

"Well, by Jeez!" The first sergeant of Headquarters Company of the five-oh-deuce was a lanky red-faced man with razor-sharp pantlegs and the gung-ho patches of airborne and combat infantry on his chest. A tattooed snake curled around his wrist and up his forearm, undulating as he rubbed his rough hands together and gloated over the nervous formation in front of him. "You're my newbies, yah? By Jeez, you're a good-lookin group! How bout them, ell-tee, ain't they a good-lookin group?"

The lieutenant was a ring-knocker; even if she hadn't seen the West Point hardware on his left hand, Nikki would have known that. His lip was rolled up like a windowshade, a sneer that said, no, they're not a good-lookin group, they look like a bunch of wannabees who couldn't make it in the civilian world so I'm stuck with them and will God tell me why? He was five-foot-nine of simmering black-haired, black-eyed machismo, a brand-new company commander with a lot to prove and not much time do it; this rack of fresh meat didn't look as if they were going to give much assistance. "I'm First Lieutenant Gouda," he barked. "Your company commander. I'm not the head cheese; not to my face or behind my back or you'll learn all about Article Fifteen of the Uniform Code of Military Justice. I run a tight company in a tight battalion in a tight brigade in a tight division, so be tight. Remember when's your six-month anniversary of being in the Army. Before it all you got to do is say you want to go home to mama and I'll let you. After it you belong to me, and Lincoln didn't free Headquarters Company of the five-oh-deuce. Just don't step on your dick and we'll get along fine. First Sergeant Czosnik'll in-process you and assign platoons and rooms."

First Sergeant Czosnik waited for the barracks door to close behind the commander before he leered a crooked grin at his formation of sixteen. "Rest," he said, and they dropped their rigid positions of attention. "Smoke em if ya got em. Yah, that's the head cheese, all right. He's a piece a work, yah?"

Most of the formation laughed. Nikki Cole watched the topkick's eyes; he saw who laughed, and looked like a man who'd remember what he saw. She'd seen the good guy-bad guy game before; she lit up and waited for what this supposed good guy might say. "Borrow your lighter, Cole?" a voice behind her whispered, and she passed it back to the tall woman with the mean game of pool and got the Zippo tucked back into her hand without so much as a brush of skin on skin.

The first sergeant talked; they listened. He took them into the barracks, crowded them into his office, and asked for papers; they gave him copies of their orders. He gloated and grinned and rubbed his hands; he said yah and let them know Gouda was the head cheese no matter what the good lieutenant thought. He doled out platoon assignments and room keys and one by one, they left his office. Nikki dragged her duffle down the first-floor hall, looking for the number on her key, and fitted it into the lock and pushed open the door to find stifling heat, two narrow beds, four big lockers, two nightstands, two chairs. "Eww. Bad hotel." First come, first served; she flopped onto the bare mattress of the bed by the wall, leaving the windows for whichever of the four other women in the group might join her.

Czosnik had given them the rest of the day to get settled, a generosity she hadn't expected. She thought of what the head cheese had said about six- month anniversaries. She had longer than six months to get out whenever she wanted, if she decided she hated it—or, if she decided it was intolerable; she already hated it. All Nikki Cole had to do was salute the man and say, "I'm a lesbian," and she'd be on the next bus out of Killeen, Texas; she had no doubt of that. She sighed and got up, and lit a smoke and went to open the windows, drawing the shades against the sun beaming into the room. She dug into her suitcase to find a clean T-shirt and the heavy crystal ashtray her brother had given her; she put her smoke in the ashtray and shed her fatigue shirt, feeling better in only the thin cotton tee under it. She was a small woman, slender and tiny-breasted, and she never wore a bra; in this heat, she knew that omission would be merciful. She scrubbed the damp T-shirt against her skin, soaking up as much sweat as she could before she changed. Maybe a shower—but there was a lot to do; she'd just get all lathered up again.

She opened the lockers, finding bedding and hangers and no more. The room was big enough for the furniture it held and the people it was to serve; the idea of one person in her space was wonderful, after being stacked forty to a bay at McClellan, and ten to a room designed for six at Dix, but it would be even more wonderful if Czosnik had neglected to assign her a roommate.

No such luck. On the heels of the thought came the sound of a key in the door. She looked up, her sweaty T-shirt half-on, half-off. "McNally. Hi."

"Cole." It wasn't quite curt, but it was several shades of warmth short of cordial as the pool player kicked in a duffle and a suitcase and slammed the door; Nikki finished peeling off her shirt, used it to towel under her arms, and pulled on the clean one. "I fucking hate Texas already," the tall woman snarled. "Jesus, this heat and it's only April? Christ, this room's hot!"

"Sucks," Nikki agreed. "Do you mind the bed by the window?" She pulled pins from her hair; a wealth of straight dark length spilled down her back.

"I couldn't give a shit. I'm on the fucking rag and I'm out of fucking smokes and—thanks." She caught the pack of Marlboro Lights Nikki tossed her. "Some bitch PFC named Trapp just gave me a ration of shit about dragging my duffle bag down the hall; did that look like a Fort Dix shine on the floor to you?" She shrugged out of her fatigue shirt and tossed it onto the bed.

"Looked like shit to me. Does that laundry list of complaints end with, and they gave me a fucking queer for a roommate?"

"I don't care who you sleep with as long as you don't come on to me. You got any aspirin? Some prick stole my cosmetic case over at the reppledepple, kiss a hundred bucks worth of makeup and Daddy's leather AWOL bag goodbye. I hope he looks good in my Mary Kay down at the 440 Light Company. And no, I'm not always this bitchy."

"Thank god." Nikki offered a bottle of aspirin. "How 'bout that Gouda? Don't step on your dick, he says. Not a problem. Czosnik's right; he's a piece of work."

"He's dangerous. You be damn careful of him, Cole. He doesn't want women in his man's army at all, let alone lesbians."

"I'm not planning on making it a career."

"The Army, or being lesbian?" Dryly, she asked; Nikki grinned. "You're food service, aren't you?"

"Yeah. I'm Nikki, by the way." She offered a hand.

"Elen." Her handshake was firm and brief. "Truck driver. First Sergeant said if it didn't work rooming a cook and a trucker together he'd move one of us. Something about you need to get up at three lots of mornings?"

"Three days a week is how we did it at Dix. Yeah, they told us the cooks always room together. I'm pretty quiet, though. I can dress in the dark."

"We'll see how it works out."

"So why'd you join the Army?" Nikki unfolded the sheets she had found in one of her lockers and snapped one out across her bunk. It smelled a little stale, but had laundry creases in it.

"One-way ticket out of Aroostook County, Maine—so I thought then. I wish I'd joined the Air Force and asked for Loring now, but the Air Force recruiter was a dork. The Navy recruiter was on leave. The Marines were like, no way."

"No shit. A few good men, right?" She made quick, neat hospital corners on the bottom sheet and flipped the top one over it. "I'm from Boston; we're almost homies, I guess. I went to Aroostook once, fishing with some friends. A place called Deboullie Pond?"

"I know Deboullie. Blueback trout. Good fly-fishing up there." She dry-swallowed three aspirin and gave the bottle back. "How come you're a lesbian?"

Nikki shrugged. "How come you're not?"

Elen laughed. "Fair question. Why'd you join up, if you're gay? You had to know they've got the deck stacked against you all the way."

"Couldn't afford any other food service education." She flipped a woolen blanket over the sheets. "God, why do they issue wool blankets in Texas?"

"Shit if I know. Shit if I'll sleep under it, either. I need a car. I need a beer. I need to bum another cigarette. I need to find the PX. I need some fucking sleep."

Nikki tossed her a fresh pack of smokes. "Keep them; I've got a carton. Do you mind if I sleep naked? It's too hot for pajamas."

"Just do it over there." She unlocked her duffle bag and started hauling things out, working into a locker; Nikki found a paperback in her suitcase and settled onto the bed, leaving her unpacking for later. Elen McNally seemed charged with nervous energy, and two of them on that end of the room would only end up in each others' way.

Elen worked her basic issue into one locker and half her footlocker, her movements as fluid as they had been across the pool table at the replacement detachment; she let the lid of the footlocker slam down and heaved her suitcase up onto it and opened it, stared in, and closed it again and sat beside it with a huge, weary sigh. "Frig it for a minute." She lit a cigarette and smoked half of it in silence before she said, "Cole?"

"Hmm?" She marked her place on the page with a finger.

"Why'd you ask me if I was gay?"

Nikki glanced up. "Error of judgment." *Wishful thinking. If you were, you'd be butch, and I'd be half in love by now.*

"Do I look queer?"

"Lots of gay people don't look gay." She put gentle emphasis on the word. "It was probably the pool cue. I had a girlfriend who was a pool player. She always wanted a stick like yours. Are you going to worry about it now?"

"No. I just wondered."

"Are you going to worry about me being your room-mate?"

"No. I'll assume you're couth unless you prove otherwise." She butted her cigarette and opened her suitcase again, wanting some of the wrinkles to hang out before she started the painstaking task of ironing everything she owned. She knew Cole was watching her, but assumed the inactive tend to watch the active just for something to do—and there was a small satisfaction in being desirable, even to another woman. In high school she'd been the fat, geeky one with the weird, perpetually-mispronounced name, dateless for four years, with only one good friend; her friend was fat and dateless too. Straight-A dorks, both of them, school paper and war protests or not. A year and a half of arduous effort and seventy-five pounds later, at five-nine and one-twenty-five she was svelte, the mirror showing a sculpted, high-cheek-boned face with expressive, almost sultry, hazel eyes, but sometimes when she looked she still saw fat and zits. Sure, the Army had been a ticket out of a desperately depressed rural county the rest of her home state barely knew existed, but it had been a chance for a fresh start, too, a chance to see how people who hadn't known her all her life might perceive her, and she'd been asked out by enough men in the last four months to make up for four lonely years of high school. To know she was seen as a tempting and mature woman instead of a fat nerd only made it easier to accept Nikki Cole's gaze at her back.

Weights, Nikki thought, watching the sinuous flow of well-toned muscles under the thin white T-shirt. *She works out with weights, plays a wicked game of pool, wears a hip-pocket wallet, and she's straight? Why doesn't this figure? I've known I'm lesbian since I was thirteen and I've never seen so obvious a dyke—but she's straight. Go fish; how do I know? But god, is she great-looking. Beautiful hands, nice tits, cute ass, ogod yummy shut up and read, Cole. She's straight, okay? Deal with it. Prove you're couth.*

CHAPTER TWO

They got along well. Elen was too feminist in her thinking and too hot in her temper to survive without sharply-honed intelligence; she had that. She came across as arrogant, almost insolent in her perpetual test of the limits of the system, daring them to prove her wrong, flirting constantly with the edges of Lieutenant Gouda's Article 15, a catch-all regulation that allowed non-judicial punishment of minor infractions of good order and discipline; she figured it a wasted week if she didn't get read her rights at least once.

Nikki, equally bright, more feminist, a veteran of the homophobia wars of high school, had left hotheadedness far behind her. She was quiet on the job but provided scathing commentary on it in the privacy of Room 104, sometimes defusing her impetuous roomie, sometimes providing her with ammunition. Nikki hated the mess hall; she wanted a restaurant. Elen hated the motor pool; she wanted to be a journalist. They both disdained most of the women in the battalion; most of the women thought they were incurable snots. They hung out because they were roomies, because they were New Englanders, because no one else liked them— and because in spite of their differences in sexuality, they enjoyed each others' company. Elen bought a car; Nikki kept it full of gas. Elen bought their beer; Nikki bought the cigarettes. They did some Saturday afternoons at Stillhouse Hollow Lake, drinking beer and smoking a little dope, Elen working on a tan and Nikki working to protect her delicately pale skin, or went to Austin to Hippie Hollow at Lake Travis, or to the malls. But weekend nights Elen dated a lot of men; Nikki had spent some time checking out the local action before resigning herself to reading a lot, keeping a light on for Elen even when it seemed a sure thing late on a Friday or Saturday night that she wouldn't make it home until sometime the next morning. "You're gonna get the clap," she grumbled at Elen one July Sunday morning, shades pulled and lights out in deference to a reportedly stupendous hangover. "Or get knocked up or something. Then what?"

"Oh, mother," Elen whispered miserably. "Leave me alone."

"What did you do in the Army, Mommy? I balled my way through an entire battalion. Elen, you're—"

"Nikki, shut up."

"Well, I care about you, you know? No one else in this place does, including that prick from A Company you were balling last night, or any of the rest of the third floor, or—"

"Fuck off, Nikki!"

The prick from A Company she'd been balling last night had succinctly proven how little he cared about her. "You an me, baby, we can make some money," he had said. "You don't care who you do it with. No sense you givin it away when they're willin to pay for it with a hot-looking bitch like you. But you got to get over sayin no to turnin over, baby. Let me break that other cherry for you. I'll make you love it—then we'll sell some."

She tried to refuse him; he overpowered her easily, laughing as he threw her across the edge of the bed to claim the small bit of virginity she had left. The cause of the hangover came later; she waited for him to pass out before she took what was left of the fifth of rum he had bought and caught a cab to the barracks to get her own car, and she drove way out onto a range road in West Fort Hood and killed the rest of the rum alone in the black night, drinking from the neck of the bottle, crying, smoking, hurt and bleeding and disillusioned. *You don't care who you do it with*—You cheap shit, she had wept, not knowing if she meant him or herself. Now, with Nikki nagging her, the tears were trying to start again; she pulled the sheet over her head, curling into a shivering ball under the thin cover. "Just leave me alone, will you? Please?"

"Elen—" Hesitantly, Nikki reached to touch Elen's shoulder, feeling the trembling ache of her under her hand. "Mac, is this more than a hangover?" Elen curled smaller into herself, one hard, rasping sob slipping from her. "Jesus, did he hurt you? Hey—" She sat on the edge of the bed. Risking the misunderstanding of her touch, she gentled the sheet away from Elen's thick, dark-blonde hair, tracing her nails through it, offering a soothing massage to the tension in the back of her roommate's neck. "I'm your friend, Elen. Maybe not as good a one or as old a one as you need, but I'm as much a one as you've got here. Please, Mac. It won't hurt so bad if you talk about it."

Elen fought a brief battle with the knowledge of Nikki's sexuality and lost; she reached desperately for her warmth, for her caring, burying her face into Nikki's belly, clinging to her. "He—Nikki, he—oh, god," she sobbed. "I feel so fucking stupid—"

Nikki held her while she cried, hating the handsome Craig Hogle with a dull ache as she whispered the soothing sounds women learn from their mothers and grandmothers: "it'll be okay," as she stroked the soft blonde hair; "it's all right, hon" as one hand massaged the slender strong shoulders; "there now, baby, there." It wasn't okay, it wasn't all right, and the endearments were only part of the ritual, but it wasn't words that mattered; it was that calming murmur that made it easier for the hard sobs to turn to hiccoughs and then sniffs, and she stretched for a tissue and tucked it into Elen's hand for when she wanted it. "Can you tell me, Elen? Did he hurt you? Please, tell me that much—"

"I hurt, but I'm not hurt." She would have used the tissue but she didn't want to move; she felt safe against the small slimness of Nikki's body, feeling her curled around her in concern, Nikki's hands gentle against her hair, against her back. "I feel so stupid," she whispered. "God, I feel so stupid—"

"No, Elen. What happened? Are you sure you aren't hurt?" When Elen had reached for her the top sheet had come with her; a frank smear of blood glared against the whiteness of the bed. "Mac, there's blood," she said gently. "Do you need a doctor?"

"No! Nikki, no—"

"Elen, if he hurt you, you need to see a doctor," she whispered. "Let me drive you over to the hospital. Please. You don't have to tell them anything if you don't want to, but—"

"No. I'm okay." She hurt, but nothing felt wrong inside; doctors meant explanations, meant MPs, meant too many things she wasn't ready to face, like Craig Hogle saying hey, she asked for it, and her trying to explain the difference between what she had asked for and what she had gotten. "It's just— oh, god." She wept quietly this time, for what he had said, not what he had done; patiently, Nikki held her, and listened when she could talk again.

"The fucking bastard," she whispered, when she heard what he had said. "Elen, don't listen to him. You're looking for something, that's all. You just don't know what. Maybe you're looking in the wrong place, but—"

"I have to listen! He's right. I might as well be selling it. I could make more money hustling my ass than hustling pool—"

"Elen—"

"—but I'm done. All the guys with their dicks in their hands waiting for a turn at me need to find a new punchboard. I'm through." She sat up, finally, paling at how much it hurt to move. "Ow—" She had to catch her breath, to measure the feel of the pain; was it more than just sore? "Don't start," she warned the uneasiness in Nikki's eyes. "I might not shit for three days, but I'm not going to the doctor." She pulled the sheet over her. "God, I don't have a stitch on—I just fell into bed last night. I'm sorry."

"What for?"

Elen smiled wanly. "Making life hard for you? Thanks, Nikki."

Nikki smiled, too, reaching to brush a hand across the short golden hair. "I don't get hard," she said gently. "And I've seen you naked before, Elen. There's a big difference between loving and wanting."

Elen looked at her. "It's not like with the guys, is it." It wasn't a question; her voice was low and hesitant. "It's way different from that."

"Way different," Nikki said softly. "Loving women is as different from the guys as we are from the other women in this shitty place, Mac. That's why I asked that day if you were gay. You're not like those catty cunts. You're like sisters. You just had that—feel about you. Like sanity."

Elen sighed, a huge and shaky sigh. "I'm beginning to
wonder if you don't have the right idea." She leaned against
the wall, pulling the sheet over her breasts, feeling the sharp,
private pain and the slow thump of the hangover; she had
puked out most of the rum, but not enough to prevent the
sodden headache and the hollow queasiness. "Don't get en-
couraged or anything, but—I just need to think about things.
Celibacy looks pretty damn good right now."

"It's always an option. Sometimes it's the best one."
Gently, she squeezed Elen's knee through the sheet. "How
about I go over to the mess hall and make you an omelet and
a canteen of coffee. You'll feel better if you eat."

"Urk. Real light on the grease, Nick."

"That's Robbie that makes the greasy omelets. I don't
even know how he does it." She stepped into her jeans.
"Fifteen minutes. You sure you're okay?"

"Sure," she whispered. "Thanks. You're a good friend,
Nikki."

Briefly, Nikki smiled. "You're worth it."

❏   ❏   ❏

Nikki Cole was a lesbian, but she knew some of the
tricks that got a man's attention, and one of them was her
voice; when she purred "Hey, big man," Craig Hogle looked
up with liquid dark eyes.

"Hey, Miss Lady." She had drop-dead looks, all pale
skin and thick dark hair and huge brown eyes, and he didn't
believe rumors until he knew them to be true; this woman was
too pretty to be queer. He offered a brilliant smile and was
rewarded with the slip of her hand across his freshly-shaven
face. He had just been amusing a table of ten with tales of his
prowess, last night figuring heavily in the telling, and this

only confirmed it; obviously, McNally had been bragging him up. "What can I do for you, sweet lady?"

"Well—" Her fingertip stroked his slim mustache, made a gentle inspection of his shave, tickled his ear. "I'd been thinking it was time we got it on, you and me," she said huskily, just loud enough for his mates to hear; they prodded elbows into each others' ribs, raised grinning eyebrows, made that suggestive male aaay-aay sound that made her skin crawl. "But if you can't get it up for Elen McNally, how could you ever get it up for me?"

She skipped lightly away from the hand he lashed at her, the hoots of his buddies ringing behind her as she escaped to the kitchen; she heard his protest and their caustic laughter and she smiled in grim satisfaction. "Tell them any different," she muttered. "I'll fucking neuter you, you prick."

"I'll fuckin' kill you, you lezzy cunt," he snarled when she came by his table again, one hand bearing Elen's breakfast between two plates, the other carrying a Thermos of coffee that had been nearly boiling when it had left the pot; there was plenty more coffee if she needed this batch for a weapon.

"Hogle, you don't have anything hard enough to hurt me with." She toasted him with the coffee, leaving him looking an unhealthy shade of purple with his mates crowing at him all over again.

Elen looked hollow-eyed and haunted when she got back to their room; she shook her head listlessly at the offer of food and accepted coffee only to wash down a trio of aspirin. "I wish you'd eat," Nikki said. "I ran a hell of a gauntlet to make this for you. The warrant officer was there, I had to lie to him, he thinks this is for the duty officer, and—"

"Piss on a guilt trip, Cole," Elen grumbled, but she accepted the fork Nikki offered with the plate, taking a cautious taste; the omelet was light, spicy with onion and

garlic, subtle with mushrooms and alfalfa sprouts from the
mess officer's private stock (he hadn't been there), dusted
with ham and sharp cheese. "Umm," she admitted, and took
another bite. "This is good, Nikki."

"Well, sure. That's my recipe, not the Army's: Nikki
Cole's famous one egg omelet, except I used two eggs." She
helped herself to coffee. "Are you going to be okay to work
in the morning?"

"Sure. I'll just crawl onto a creeper under a truck and
sleep all day. I won't love it, but I'll survive it." She speared
the last slice of mushroom from the plate, surprised the omelet
was gone; she hadn't suspected she was hungry. "You're a
good cook, Nikki. Thanks."

"No sweat. The warrant wasn't really there. Just Robbie, and he doesn't give a shit. He's a good guy."

"Yeah," Elen murmured; she had slept with him, too,
and enjoyed it; he had been a kind, gentle lover, asking shyly
if she would consider being his girl. She set the plate on the
nightstand and settled back against the pillows with her
coffee. More than anything she wanted a shower, but she had
tried to get up and had been afraid she might faint before she
made it to the door, let alone the twenty steps down the hall
to the latrine. It was one thing to ask for Nikki's help; it was
another to think of who might be hanging around out in the
hall to witness her need for that assistance. She could hear the
Sunday-lazy flow of the barracks out there, the shuck-and-
jive of half a dozen bored men at the Bravo charge of quarters
desk twenty feet away, the parade of cowboy-booted feet
passing their door on the way to the dayroom on the Alpha
end of the building; the topkick said women were housed on
the first floor for their own protection, but right now she'd
have given a lot to live upstairs, where a degree of privacy
might have been possible. "Oh, boy," she sighed. "Nikki, I

gotta pee, and I don't know if I can make it down there myself. And god, I want a shower. I need to wash his stink off me."

"I'll go with you, but you're going to do it yourself." Elen's dread of being a spectator sport was too clear. "You're a soldier, eh? Prove it now. It's twenty steps. Do it with your head up, Mac, and don't ever let that prick know he hurt you. You can get in there and fall out and I'll catch you, but you're going to get there proud."

"You've got more faith in me than I do," Elen muttered, and Nikki shot her a look of good-humored disgust and got her robe from her locker; she helped her out of bed and into the robe and as far as their door, and let her rest there. "Okay," Elen whispered. "Here goes nothing."

"Just remember Trapp and her gang are at church. That's six obstacles overcome in one fell swoop. Forward march, troop. You don't remember pain once it's over with. All you've got to do is put yourself ahead of it."

Put yourself ahead of it— It was weird, but it worked; she thought herself there and was there. The latrine was mercifully empty, and she leaned on the wall inside that door and shivered, sweating, trying to keep Nikki's excellent omelet in her stomach. "Oh, boy. Would you forgive me if I puked?"

"I'll leave you to fucking drown if you puke," she threatened, and snugged an arm around her to support her to a shower stall. "Piss in the shower," she grumbled, when Elen protested of that need. "It's A Company's turn to clean the latrine. Any of those bitches your buddies?"

"You're gross, Cole. You're really rude."

"I know. Holler if you need me. You don't think I'm going in there with you, do you? Church doesn't last forever, and that's all Trapp would need to see, us in the same shower. We'd be civilians by Friday."

"What a wonderful thought. Come on in, the water's great."

"You know you love the Army."

"Fuck the Army."

She stayed under the spray for a long time, letting it cleanse her, soothe her; she soaped three times and washed her hair twice, and felt better by the time she twisted off the taps and Nikki poked her towel around the curtain, and the walk back to the room was easier. She was even able to exchange a greeting with Jeannie Kincaid, the only other woman in the battalion she liked at all, when they met in the hall. "Woo. Rough night, Mac?"

"Demon rum," Elen smiled wanly. "I'm a hurtin' unit."

"Stick with toke," Jeannie grinned, palming her a slender joint. "Beats hair of the dog, for sure. This is nice and easy. Heal the pain."

"A true pal. Thanks, Jeannie." She looked hungrily at the joint, back in the room. "Don't I wish I dared." But she gave it to Nikki, who stretched on tiptoe on her bed to pop up a panel of the suspended ceiling, tucking it with the rest of their small stash while Elen got out of her robe and into a T-shirt and panties and started to get back into bed. "Uck," she said at sheets still damp with sweat and blood, and Nikki stripped the bed and made it fresh with the grim efficiency of nurses and mothers and soldiers. "I could have done that," Elen protested.

"No doubt, but it's done. Get in. Anything else you need, while I'm in a mood to wait on you?"

She shook her head and curled into the crisp, clean sheets. She wanted to sleep and was afraid to try, afraid the thinking would crowd in at her, haunt her, fill her dreams. "Nikki—" The room was hot, but she shivered. "Could you stick around a while? I don't want to be alone."

"I'll be right here," she said quietly. "Try to get some sleep."

She was clean, and safe, and Nikki was there; the aspirin was dulling the pain. Exhaustion slipped in to take her.

Nikki watched her sleep for a long, long time before she sighed softly and found one of her endless string of paperbacks; settling onto her own bed with it, she read. Every now and then she glanced at Elen, listening to the slow breaths of her sleeping. A few times she recalled the look on Craig Hogle's face when she'd said "you don't have anything hard enough to hurt me with," and a tiny, cold smile touched her. She wasn't through with him yet. By the time she was, he'd be lucky if he ever got it up again.

CHAPTER THREE

Major Kare Dillinger studied the pair of boots attached to the pair of legs attached to someone under a two-and-a-half ton truck in the Headquarters Company Third Platoon line of the five-oh-deuce motor pool. The boots and the legs had been in this cross-ankled position when she had come up the line; twenty minutes later, they didn't appear to have moved. She knew that on a 105-degree day in a Fort Hood motor pool, the coolest place in seventy-five acres was the shade under a truck. The major didn't mind a little shamming; she even respected creative goldbricking, but there was no creativity in sleeping under a deuce-and-a-half, and she purely hated seeing Corcoran jump boots with the silver balls of a dogtag chain poked into the holes across the toes. These boots had those balls, and she had a pretty good idea that if she dragged this GI out from under she'd find some small-footed, big-pupilled Latino troop whose name was prominent on her list of suspected dopers. With an utter lack of regard for the painstaking spit-shine on those beaded boots, she slapped a palm onto each toe and pulled.

"Jesus frigging Chr—ouch! Oh shit Jesus! What stupid son of a whore—"

"Oh, hell," said the major. This was no small-footed Latino. This was a female snuffy she had handled so roughly,

24

now bleeding with the profusion only scalp wounds can deliver, having sat up abruptly when the major grabbed and yanked, colliding with some part of the transmission with force enough to split her forehead in good shape. "Jesus, McNally, I'm sorry—"

"You numb shit!" Elen held her head, blood dripping between her fingers, queasy from that and the awakened effects of Saturday night's abuse. "What the fuck is your problem—" She peeked between her fingers to see sun glinting on burnished-copper hair that could only belong to the Executive Officer. "Oops. Ma'am?"

"Oops, indeed," the major smiled, hunkering down beside her. "Let me look." Her handkerchief was Monday-morning clean; she pressed it to the cut. "You might need a stitch or two, McNally. I can't tell you how sorry I am—"

"I know you're sorry," she muttered, and the major knew the rest of it: *now apologize.* McNally shook off the hand she offered, getting up her own way, unable to hide how much it hurt to do it; Dillinger made ready to catch her if she fainted. "God, I'm really bleeding, here—"

"PJ!" the major hollered; her driver trotted up, saw the blood, and hustled for the jeep.

The major stayed with her at the hospital while an almost elderly physician placed six neat, tiny stitches on the cut before chasing Dillinger away so he could ask Elen what else was wrong with her. She didn't move the way he thought a healthy nineteen-year-old woman should move.

"Nothing, sir," she stonewalled. "Bad back."

"I'm a gynecologist," he said gently. "And a civilian."

"Sure, and you'll call the MPs just as quick as a regular army medic. Thanks anyway. I'll heal."

"Between us, then. No MPs. I know how much tender loving care they give rape victims. I'd just like to make sure you're all right."

She huffed a defeated sigh; whether he had seen it in her eyes or how she moved, he knew. "Okay," she whispered, and allowed his examination; he was gentle, waiting when she tightened in apprehension or in pain, and while she dressed he went to the pharmacy and got a tube of the same cooling salve he had applied and told her how to use it. He didn't ask who or how or anything but when; he didn't say she should report it; he didn't lecture her. He treated her, advised no intercourse for two weeks, and handed her over to her Executive Officer with a profile for three days of bed rest and two weeks of light duty, and squeezed her shoulder gently and tossed her chart in a box and said to the sergeant behind the Emergency Room desk, "Who's next?"

"Female soldiers," she heard Lieutenant Gouda sneer in the hallway outside her room in the barracks, just before she drifted off. "Two weeks of light duty for a bump on the head a man wouldn't even have noticed?"

"Keep your opinions to yourself, mister, until you get a medical degree," Major Dillinger snapped, and Chuckie Cheeseballs opened his mouth to retort, remembered this female soldier seriously outranked him and had him at a disconcerting height disadvantage as well, and shut it again.

"Send her up to the head shed for her light duty." The doctor had taken her aside at the hospital to tell her the profile wasn't for the bump on the head; he suggested that emotional wreckage from the rape might be salved by a few weeks away from the coarse repartee of the motor pool. "If she can type, I'll keep her."

Elen smiled; she could type, all right. She could smoke out about seventy words a minute. She went to sleep liking the Executive Officer even if she had scarred her face for life. She always wore her hair over her forehead anyway.

❏   ❏   ❏

"The Executive Officer? The XO? Jesus, are you kidding? She breaks my heart," Nikki mourned. "She's so fucking gorgeous, but no slack or what! You ever been in her office? There's a sign on her desk that says, 'The Army Gets Better Every Time A Doper Gets Busted.'"

"And PJ's her driver? She's blind or kidding, Nikki. I buy all my grass from PJ. And she was really nice today."

"She was wrong today. She had to be nice. You'll be working with Trapp," Nikki warned. "And Captain Guzman? He gives me the creeping willies."

"No worse than Cheeseballs. And Jeannie works up there; she's okay." Elen settled into the pillows with a huge yawn; the doctor had prescribed Percodan. It had given her a gentle buzz, like the contact high from someone else's good dope. She was enjoying that little buzz—and knowing that Hogle hadn't ripped her up inside. When the bleeding hadn't stopped this morning she had been glad Nikki was on the breakfast shift; there'd have been no way to convince her she was okay. Now she was glad shift rotation had Nikki off tomorrow and not due in Wednesday until three. Her presence in the room was quieting, calming. She remembered her dismay when First Sergeant Czosnik had told her who she'd be rooming with; to tolerate a lesbian in the barracks was one thing, but to room with one was something else again, she'd thought. But Nikki had never made a move, never touched her in any way that might be construed as suggestive, and Elen didn't want to know what it might have been like yesterday to have Julie Trapp or Pam Iver for a roommate. Just the thought made her shiver. Tin-plated cunts, Nikki called them, and Elen knew there would have been no sympathy from them. There would have been plenty of sneering, lots of you-asked-for-it derision, heaping doses of moralizing and probably a ration of Bible-reading tossed in to spice their vicious pot, but there surely would have been no gentle arms to hold her while she cried, no tolerance, no help—no love.

Way different. She could almost hear Nikki's soft voice. *Loving women is as different as we are from the other women in this place, Elen; that's why I asked you that day if you were gay. You just had that feel about you.*

Her sigh was deep and shaky; Nikki asked if she was okay. "I'm tired," she whispered. "Just—tired." She thought of all the men she had allowed between her legs in the last months and turned toward the windows, away from Nikki, hiding the tears. *Never again. Never, never, never . . .*

Nikki let her cry. Some tears, she knew, were not for sharing.

❏   ❏   ❏

She watched Craig Hogle as he worked his way through the chow line: he showed his meal card, signed the sheet, and slouched hands in pockets, sullen against the ribbing of his mates; he looked like a man who desperately wished he had money enough three days before payday to eat downtown. "Hey, Hogle," she crooned, when he was in front of her, and he looked up, simmering with a hatred that was almost physical. "Talked to a cook from the Maintenance the other day. Juanita?" She had; if Juanita could be believed, Hogle had promised her the time of her life before getting so stoned he couldn't give her the time of day. She hovered tongs over the tray of chicken in front of her. "Let's see. You look like a tit man to me." Delicately, she selected a breast of chicken and dropped it to his tray. "Maybe we should have oysters for you, hombre."

"Give it a break," he gritted. "I'll fuck you up, Cole."

"You can fuck up all right enough, Hogle," she grinned. "You just can't fuck." She let her eyes laugh at him; he was quivering with impotent rage. "Unless you fight better than you fuck, don't try me, Hogle. I could relieve you of your useless dick in ten seconds and you'd never get a lick in. Even if licking's all you've got to work with—"

"You fucking bitch!" He heaved his tray at her. She had expected that, and ducked; food sprayed across the kitchen behind her. He launched over the counter, kicking chicken and mashed potatoes out of his way, but before the cooks on either side of her had time to react, she had him screaming in pain and harboring a pure terror that she would rip his scrotum out through the cloth of his pants.

"Big man," she said with awful contempt, keeping a merciless grip on him as he paled to ashen grey, a keen of anguish seeping from his throat; her voice was soft, meant for him only. "She never would've hurt you. You fucked up, man, hurting her." She twitched her wrist enough to make him believe his balls were leaving him now; his eyes rolled back and she let him go. He sobbed to his knees in front of her, reaching with both hands for the wounded part of him. He would be much lamer much longer than Elen would be; Nikki had long, hard fingernails and enough rage to have broken three of them when she clamped onto him. He could feel warm blood running down his thighs. "Can't fuck and can't fight," she said, giving it enough volume to ensure the tale she wanted told would be, "and not enough brains not to try either one. I'm five foot three, I weigh a hundred and two pounds, and I put you on your fucking knees."

The battalion commander was on leave; she ended up in front of Major Dillinger's desk to tell her side of the story. She stonewalled her; the major sighed and told her to sit down, and leaned back in her chair. "I know what happened to Elen McNally Saturday night," she said quietly. "That makes us and whatever son of a bitch did it—and the doctor—the only ones to know, and I'll keep it that way if that's what Elen wants. All I want to know is if the right son of a bitch got a lesson today."

Nikki's smile was brief and cold. "Only if he's smart enough to learn."

Dillinger smiled, too. "I hear you fight pretty good for a little girl."

"I'm a small woman, Major," she said quietly. "I'm not a little girl."

❏   ❏   ❏

All she ever wanted when she left the mess hall was a shower. Air conditioning couldn't keep the sweat from pouring from the cooks, and nothing kept the grease from sticking to the sweat. She could smell the difference today: putting the squeeze to Hogle had been savage, almost sexual, and the dintinction was there to her nose, sharp, caustic; there'd been a tang of raw nervousness in presenting herself to the major, and that bitter scent of danger was there, too. The men in the barracks fell silent, making way in resentment and uneasy respect when she entered. Her teasing Hogle had been okay when it was teasing, but it had stopped being funny when she made him scream. "Ol' Ballbuster," she heard, a murmur behind her. She sighed and tried the door; it was locked. She slipped her key into the knob, hoping there was enough ice left in the cooler to have kept that one last brew cool enough to drink.

"What the fuck did you have to do that for? Jesus Christ, Nikki! Why not just publish it in the fucking *Sentinel*? God, I trusted you—"

She leaned wearily against the door. "Elen, can I have a shower before we have our first fight? I'm just not ready for the third round yet."

"Why couldn't you leave it alone? I've spent two hours listening to them laughing at me out there, Nikki! God—"

Nikki stripped out of her uniform and tossed it at a basket in the corner; she tugged on a T-shirt that hung to her knees, plucked towel and soap and shampoo from her locker, jammed her feet into shower shoes, and paused at the door. "They're not laughing at you, they're laughing at him. Maybe I didn't do it just for you. Maybe I did it for me, and Jeannie Kincaid, and even Scuzball Trapp and her slimy gang. Maybe I was just making a fucking statement?"

She slammed the door behind her and wished she hadn't when the scuzball Julie Trapp, there in the hall to hear at least part of it, most probably her own reference, smiled with sweet acidity. "Lover's quarrel, Cole? Tsk, tsk. Go get that cold shower. Sounds like you'll need it."

"Goodness and mercy might follow you all the days of your life, Trapp, but they'll never fucking catch up with you." Nikki slapped down the hall in her shower shoes to slam open the latrine door.

"Way to go, Nick," Jeannie Kincaid crowed around a mouthful of toothpaste. "That prick's had it coming for two years I know about." She spat and rinsed. "I hear you had him screaming at your feet. I'm so pissed I didn't see it, man, it must have been fucking great! What'd the major say?"

Nikki hung her robe on a hook and stacked her shower stuff in a stall. She kind of liked Jeannie, even if she was straight as a Kansas country road. "He came at me. I defended myself. What's to say?"

"Well, yeah. But you've been ragging his butt hard."

"Don't matter. You can only respond with like force. That's the rules, according to the Queen of Marksbury or someone." She turned on the hot water and waited for it to come up. "So he's got eight inches and eighty pounds on me? I just grabbed the eight inches and squeezed." She stepped into the shower to the sound of Jeannie's laughter. It made her feel better.

Elen wasn't in the room when she got back; she blew an exasperated sigh. She hadn't looked forward to the fight, only to being on the finished end of it, and she knew waiting would churn her into knots. That last beer was warm. "Shit." She found a set of surgical scrubs in her footlocker, neatly pressed and folded: Elen's work. Keeping uniforms clean and creased was a major chore; keeping the room inspection-ready was equally time-consuming. Nikki satisfied the white glove of the head cheese, and Elen kept them crisply starched. It had occurred to her how much being roommates was like a marriage; until today, theirs had been a good one. Elen ripping into her and then running from resolution hurt, and pissed her off.

She sighed again, glaring at the handsome maple bookcase Elen had made for her one night while holding down the charge of quarters desk. CQ was long and boring duty; the wood was sanded satin-smooth, edges softened, screws counter-sunk and pegged, details of completion that had kept Elen awake all night after all day in the heat of the motor pool—so she had said. That she'd done it at all touched Nikki deeply; that she'd done such a caring job of it proved more to Nikki than Elen seemed willing to admit in words.

She settled cross-legged onto the bed with one of her endless string of paperbacks and found her place. The scrubs felt cool and crisp on her skin. She wouldn't have bothered to iron them; Elen bothered. "Damn it, Mac," she murmured, "will you come home so we can talk? I love you, but I hate this."

She couldn't concentrate. She racked the book and smoked and waited. It was half an hour before she heard a key in the door; Elen came in with a brown paper bag and an uncertain smile. "Hi." She offered the bag; Nikki peeked in to find a sweating four-pack of Grolsch beer and a huge sack of cheese curls, her favorite junk food. "I'm sorry, Nick," Elen said quietly. "You said something I didn't have the guts to say, and I was too busy feeling sorry for myself to see it. Thank you—for castrating him in public, and for shaking me awake. We both deserved it. And I'm really sorry I jumped on you."

"I'm sorry I thought you were avoiding the fight," Nikki admitted. "You didn't have to do all this." She touched the bag.

"I know you like a beer after work. Are we friends again?"

"Never stopped. How're you feeling?"

"Comme ci, comme ça." She sat cross-legged at the foot of Nikki's bed and accepted a beer, figuring out the ceramic stopper. "You had this before? I asked the guy at the package store what the best beer he had was. He said this was it, if—" She looked up; Nikki was giving her a small, odd smile. "What?"

"You're a sweetheart, Elen," she said gently. "That was a really sweet thing to do. I love you even if you are straight."

Elen blushed. "Why? I mean, I love you too, Nick, but what's the big deal about some beer? It was just a thought, you know?"

"Not just some beer, Mac. You made sure you got the best? For me? And an apology? Some people might have come up with one or the other, but not many would give up both. It's just really sweet that you did."

"Nikki, if I just go around hurting you, am I any better than Hogle?"

"Did you get any flowers from him? He knows why I did what I did, but he doesn't think he deserved it. He doesn't think he was wrong, and even if he did he'd never admit it. You can. That's why I love you." She reached to ruffle a hand across Elen's hair. "Now I've embarrassed you. I'm sorry."

"No. I just—" Nikki's fingers were cool against the back of her neck, a gentle pressure there and gone; she caught the retreating hand in her own. "It just feels so different to me, Nikki, to be able to hear you say that—and to be able to say it myself. I love my friend Anne back home, but I can't say it. If I did, she'd think I was queer." A smile twitched to her. "I'm still not. But I can love you, can't I?"

As softly as Nikki's hand had brushed her hair, her lips brushed Elen's, a startling warmth gone before Elen could catch it—or know she wanted to. "Sorry; I had to do it. It's got nothing to do with queer. And lose that word for me, will you, babe?" It was a request, and a lifeline; she had felt the quick response of Elen's lips against hers, and saw the bewilderment in the hazel eyes. "I hate it. Gay, dyke or lesbian, yes; queer, homo and fag, no. Now let's see if this really is the best beer in the world while it's still cold."

CHAPTER FOUR

Lieutenant Colonel Buckman and Major Dillinger kept a close eye on Elen McNally during her stint of light duty at the head shed. Her keyboard skill was worth keeping, but her hair-trigger temper was worth watching; she snapped at Iver here and growled at Trapp there, but Trapp and Iver weren't favorites of either officer. Most of the clerks—nearly all white and female—treated the majority contingent of black male troops with arrogant condescension; Buckman overheard Elen muttering to herself at the soda machine one day: "fuckin' women're nothing but white supremacist Nazis." At the coffee pot a few days later, when Trapp said Jeannie Kincaid was proof of why North Carolina should be called the roundheel rather than the Tarheel state, Elen said quietly, "You know, Julie, someday you'll need a friend and not be able to find one," and shot Dillinger a look that clearly said, *it's not my place to stop this, but it sure as hell could be yours.* The major, who'd gotten her heels locked and her butt chewed by colonels and generals in the last fifteen years, had never felt as chastised as she did by McNally's silent reproach. She ordered Iver and Trapp into her office and kicked some serious ass, and took odd satisfaction in the tiny smile she got when she emerged; it irritated her to feel rewarded by the approval of a private. "I need that Maintenance SOP yesterday," she snapped, and got seventeen legal-size, single-spaced pages delivered late that afternoon, with a smile that was maddening in its knowledge of why she had snapped, and what that had and hadn't meant.

Jeannie Kincaid enjoyed solid footing as the battalion's far-and-away best typist, but Jeannie was on leave, and Colonel Buckman had Officer Evaluation Reports due. He called McNally into his office. "I can't stress enough the importance of confidentiality on these OERs, Elen. If you repeat—"

"Sir, I won't."

He gave her the OERs. She was back in minutes with drafts and thesaurus in hand. "I'm probably out of line, sir, but I know OERs are so important—"

"I'm no writer. If you are, talk to me." His smile put her at ease.

"You used the word outstanding four times in eleven lines, sir; I know it's a major buzzword, but redundancy reduces its impact. If you tried superlative, unparalleled or sterling, that'd be subliminal advertisement for the silver bar, and you're recommending promotion."

"Let's try this, Mac," the commander said. "You know what I want to say. You say it the way I wish I could and we'll have a look at it."

An hour later he compared what he had written with what she had typed; her changes were subtle, elevating his narratives to paragraphs more polished, more persuasive. He called division headquarters and requested Elen McNally's personnel file.

He browsed. Third in a high school class of more than three hundred, with an IQ of 146; that was uncommonly high in the all-volunteer Army of 1976. Squad and then platoon leader at Fort McClellan during Basic; same at Dix. She'd

maxxed the physical training test at McClellan; likewise at
Dix. She qualified expert with the M-16, shooting two hundred ninety-six out of three hundred—given faulty targets,
theoretically she might have shot perfectly. A photocopy of
a handwritten note from her company commander at Dix said,
"Get this soldier into OCS or West Point. Definite officer
material." She had refused a suggested appointment to West
Point.

"Take a look at this," he said to Dillinger, offering the
file across her desk, and he waited while she skimmed through
it. "DeLong's short," he said when she looked up, impressed.
"This kid can handle Jerry; I want her in that slot. Wave the
Point at her again while you're at it."

"McNally, front and center!" she called; McNally re-
ported. "Chip DeLong's a sixty-day loss. You interested in
his job?" Jerry Guzman, the operations officer, was the second most feared and disliked officer in the battalion—she
herself held top honors and knew it. He was opinionated,
conceited, and often verbally abusive of his clerks, and after
two weeks at headquarters, McNally had to know that.

But Elen's consideration was brief. "Why not? It beats
the motor pool."

"Sit down, McNally," she offered, and waited for Elen
to settle into the comfortable chair across her desk. "I'm
curious. Given all the military occupational specialties available, why did you choose to be a truck driver?"

"All the MOSs available?" McNally snorted a laugh.
"My recruiter said, with these scores you can do anything you
want. I asked for public information. He says, training's full.
So I said, how about cartography? Full. Draftsman? Full.
Clerk/Typist? We're trying to steer women away from stereo-
typical women's roles. So what've you got? I asked, and he

said truckin' or cookin'. I said trucking, and guess what. Welcome back to the stereotype."

"Would you prefer to go back to the motor pool?"

"Not at all, ma'am. I just appreciate the irony."

"Why did you turn down West Point?"

Elen gave her a tiny smile. "I joined the Army because I knew I wasn't ready for college, Major. If I wasn't ready for the University of Maine, I'm surely not ready for West Point."

"I think you might surprise yourself."

"I don't want it, ma'am," Elen said quietly.

"Why not?"

"You hauled me out from under a truck and I came out cussing you before I knew who you were. I wouldn't last a month at West Point, ma'am. I'd tell some senior right where he could put his yo-plebe crap and be a civilian by Friday."

"The fact that you recognize that makes me wonder if you're right to think it, Elen. I think you've got a lot of the qualities that make a good officer, and believe me, they'd teach you to curb that temper."

"Major Dillinger, I'm nineteen years old. I don't want to sign away ten years of my life to anyone, let alone an outfit I don't particularly like."

"It's a lot different on this side of the desk, Elen. The Army for an officer bears almost no resemblance to the Army for an enlisted person."

"Yeah, I see that," Elen said softly. "That's one of the reasons I don't like it, ma'am. Ever read *The Caine Mutiny*? Lieutenant Keefer accused the Navy of being a master plan designed by geniuses for execution by idiots. He said it was a third-rate career for third-rate people, offering skimpy security in exchange for twenty or thirty years of polite penal servitude. I'm not so sure the Army's all that much different."

The major smiled thinly. "Does it occur to you the deep offense I might take at that statement, Private McNally?"

"Would I last at West Point? There's exceptions to every rule, ma'am, and you and Colonel Buckman are exceptions. You guys are good. You care. You're rare. This place doesn't know how lucky it is to have you both at once."

Dillinger eyed her. "I'll accept that as a good recovery if nothing else. Go back to work, McNally. Report to Captain Guzman Monday morning."

"Yes, ma'am," McNally said, subdued; the major knew the private thought she'd said too much too frankly. She sat there after Elen left, wondering why this kid—*kid? I don't think so*—thought she wasn't ready for college. Intelligence and maturity sure as hell weren't the issues.

❏   ❏   ❏

"What else, sir?" Elen had just submitted next week's training schedules for Captain Guzman's approval. He'd tied into DeLong and Iver often enough in her first week, but had been fine with her; she wondered if she was being protected from above or if he just liked her work.

"Check your in box. This looks real good," he added, an afterthought.

"Thank you. My in box is clear, sir."

"Well—" He frowned at her; Chip DeLong never got training schedules in before three in the afternoon—but then, it took Chip until ten to come down from his after-formation buzz, and he couldn't find his ass or his keyboard with both hands when he was stoned. "Ask Sergeant Perry what he's got."

"I did, sir. He said ask you."

"Well, then, just look busy, for Christ's sake. Do something."

Faintly, Elen smiled. "Yes sir."

"Dear Mom and Dad," she typed, and rambled on for four pages.

"Dear Anne," she typed, and told Anne all the things she'd told her folks, with considerably more sarcasm and profanity. She folded the letters into envelopes and looked at the clock. "Can I go to lunch, Sergeant Perry?"

"Good-bye."

There was a letter in her in box when she got back. She typed it up and returned draft and final to the Captain. "Anything else, sir?"

"Just look busy, McNally. Consider it a standing order."

"Christ," Elen grumbled to Nikki that night, picking kimchee out of the rice in her plate of take-out Korean. "I ought to write a book. I've sure as hell got time enough up there."

"Go for it," Nikki grinned. "I'll edit your first drafts for you."

❑   ❑   ❑

There were things she enjoyed, things that gave her depth and serenity, a sense of inner calm so profound it made her ache in that desperate, helpless way new love makes one ache, a pain of growth and substance.

Kare Dillinger read the first few lines on the paper in the carriage of Elen McNally's typewriter. Caught, she lifted the bail to read it all, only mildly guilty; the words were personal, but not private.

She wondered if it was the fly-fishing so much as the getting to where she did it most often, that silent glide across a sunset reflected on a still pond; it was like slipping over a mirror, her senses bewildered by the duality of going across what she was going toward. Sometimes the moose was there. Most always the loons echoed their shivering songs in the gathering dusk. It was nurture for her anima to listen to the loon and the liquid slice of the blade of her paddle through the mirror. Up by the lily pads, a fish (a trout, no matter what it really was) rose and her blood stirred as if the fish were a lover she approached for the first time, the questions the same questions about chases and captures and which was really the thrill.

She read it again, wishing there was more. There was a sheet of glass on the surface of the clerk's desk; inevitably, under that glass were scraps of Elen's life, and the major studied them: a few comics cut from the paper that made her smile. A black-and-white snapshot of a handsome young man leaning on an old Chevy, beer in hand, an exultant grin on his face; Dad the day I was born, said the edge. A photo of a much heavier McNally and an older woman—her mother?—can-canning in the surf of a white-sand beach. A typewritten quote:

The discipline which makes the soldiers of a free country reliable in battle is not to be gained by harsh or tyrannical treatment. On the contrary, such treatment is far more likely to destroy than make an Army. It is possible to impart instruction and give commands in such a manner and in such a tone of voice to inspire in the soldier no feeling but an intense desire to obey, while the opposite manner and tone of voice cannot fail to excite strong resentment and a desire to disobey. The one mode or the other of dealing with subordinates springs from a corresponding spirit in the breast of the commander. He who feels the respect which is due others cannot fail to inspire in them regard for himself, while he who feels, and hence manifests, disrespect toward others, especially his subordinates, cannot fail to inspire hatred against himself.
    —Major General John M. Schofield, commencement address, West Point, 1879.

She shook her head with a resigned sigh and read the fishing-words again, and looked up to see Elen watching her from the door. "You write well."

"Thank you," Elen said, sipping at her coffee.

"I want you to read *The Art of War* by Sun Tzu. He starts from the premise that to win without fighting is best. I'll bring you my copy tomorrow."

"Thank you, ma'am."

"Given any more thought to West Point?"

"No more than I need to to know I still don't want to go."

"You'd make a good officer, Elen."

"You can't be good at anything your heart isn't in, Major."

"Point taken. Type me up a copy of this Schofield quote, would you?"

When she brought up the Point again, Elen's look said, I'll be polite with my no this time, but you're starting to get on my nerves; back off.

The third time, McNally said quietly, "Sun Tzu said the important thing in a military operation is victory, not persistence, Major Dillinger."

❏   ❏   ❏

Craig Hogle never returned to the Deuce from the hospital. His roommate packed his gear, the MPs picked it up, and he and it took a long plane ride to Korea, where he would have eighteen miserable months to contemplate the cost of that particular dip of his wick. He was soon forgotten; after a while, the only time his name arose was in conjunction with Nikki. "The day BB Cole laid the squeeze to ol' Hogle" became a milepost of sorts in battalion history, a way to gauge time done in the Deuce: were you here for Gallant Crew?

D'you remember Cap'n Mears from A Company? Were you
there the day Cole put the squeeze to ol' Hogle? No?? Man,
she gave him a field vascetomy right in the fuckin' mess hall
at suppertime. Whatever happened to him, anyway? Didn't
she make him scream. Ol' Ballbuster Cole, yeah; ol' BB.
      She learned to answer to it. Only Elen called her Nikki
anymore. She hated it, and knew she might as well hate her
brown eyes for all she could change them. She hated the mess
hall, the Deuce, Fort Hood, the Army, Texas—Elen was all
that kept her there. Room 104 was a haven where wisecracks
and insults and laughs flew between them, where if she pulled
late shift there was always a cold beer waiting even if it wasn't
Grolsch (but often it was), where on really crappy days there
might be a soothing back rub from lithe and talented hands,
stronger now for Elen's permanent position at the hard-keyed
old Remington typewriter in the operations shop at battalion
headquarters.
      The massages were a luxury, and a trial: they had started
with a complaint of a headache, and those hands had eased
the tension from her neck. A few days later she slipped at
work; her back throbbed for days until Elen said, "Christ,
Cole, you're too bitchy to live with. Lay down and I'll work
that out for you. Take your shirt off; I'm not fighting that."
Gentle fingers walked down her spine until they found a place
that made her jump; Elen worked out the worst of the stiffness
and planted the heels of her hands on either side of her spine
and pushed. There was the explosive pop of a thoracic verte-
bra snapping into place, and the hard pain was gone. A week
later was a low menstrual backache; "I'll work that out for
you." Her hands were gentle, neutral; both her parents had
bad backs, she said, and she'd learned to use her hands to ease
those pains. There was no suggestion in her touch; she meant
to soothe, and did it well. But it was hard for Nikki to be

neutral with Elen's thighs straddling her hips and long-fingered hands working cocoa butter into her skin; the fantasy was low-grade but constant: this time her hands would become a slow caress; this time she'd lean to press firm breasts against her naked back, slip her mouth across her skin, whisper *I can't hide it anymore Nikki I want you—*

"God, Nick, relax. You're really tense tonight." Elen's hands paused on her shoulders. They had taken a range road to Blackwell Mountain, smoking a joint and splitting a pint of vodka, and still Nikki was moody and quiet: Elen was a good friend, but not a gay friend, and she wasn't a lover, and sitting by the mesa sharing a pint with Elen she had tried to imagine finding a lover in the handful of dykes she knew here and couldn't, for when she tried to picture it the only body she could see with her, the only face, the only hands, the only lips and hair and eyes she could see were Elen's, and she shouldn't have allowed the massage tonight because the feel of Elen was almost unbearable; she was tense because under the pillow her hands were fisted trying to keep from reaching for Elen.

Gentle, strong, one of Elen's hands stroked the back of her neck. "Let go, Nikki. God, you'll hurt yourself staying so tight. Come on; it's Friday. You've got all weekend off." Her voice was as gentle as the hands smoothing easy circles up her ribs *Nikki, let it go*, finding a place at the small of her back that made the breath catch in her *loosen up, Nikki, let go*, working up her sides, perilously close to her breasts until they found her shoulders to soothe the knotted muscles there *help me a little, hon, feel it* and she leaned into her work—and what Nikki felt was how Elen's thighs tightened against her, how fingers caught the sides of her breasts, the brush of that warm pelvis against her rump; she felt her own helpless surge of response. "Elen, stop—" It was almost a moan. "Elen, I can't stand this, it's too—Mac, stop. Please."

"Nikki, what—oh, god." She didn't recoil. She simply slipped away from her, breaking the contact as easily as she had initiated it. Nikki could feel her presence on the narrow bed, and knew she was sitting cross-legged at the end of it. "Nikki, I'm sorry," Elen whispered. "I didn't—I never think of that. I just think of you as my friend. I didn't think—I didn't know . . ."

Helplessly, the words trailed off into a silence that stretched long and thin. Sweet, cloying, the smell of cocoa butter filled Nikki's awareness. "Oh, Nikki. God, I'm so sorry. I didn't mean to—"

Her T-shirt was in a pile by her pillow; Nikki slipped it on, and tiredly, she sat on the edge of the bed, unable to face Elen, unable to see what might be in those hazel eyes. "Elen, it's not your fault. I thought I could handle it." Her throat felt close and tight with the promise of tears. "Is this going to fuck things up with us? I can leave, Elen, I can—"

"Nikki, no! Don't say that, we can work around it—"

"How? Elen, I want you! I want you to touch me, I want you to kiss me, I want you to make love to me, how can we work around that? You're straight and I'm gay and it worked for a while but I lost control of it and I can't turn it off! Can you live with me, knowing I feel that way about you? Can you be comfortable with that?"

"I—" She remembered one brief brush of Nikki's lips against hers three months ago, remembered thinking about it for hours and days, knew that when it had happened she might have been ready for more—and she remembered how hurt she had been, how needing of someone's—anyone's—love. "It'd be hard," she said softly. "Worse for you than me. God, this isn't fair! I do love you, just—not that way. I can't—and it's not you not being fair, it's just—"

"It just isn't fair. Life sucks and then you die." She leaned elbows on knees, her head in her hands, her hair falling to hide her face; she shivered, trying not to cry. "I guess I was hoping," she said softly. "When you gave up men, I thought maybe—I'm not trying to talk you into anything, Elen, I—"

"I know. Nikki, I know. I never thought I'd say I wish I was—"

"Don't, Elen, Jesus! don't say that, don't break my fucking heart for me, okay? Christ, I feel like such a shit—"

"Nikki, don't! God, this is so hard—don't pull away from me, Nikki, you held me when I cried, you could be there for me, why—"

"I had a handle on it then, Mac! You were just my roommate then, I didn't know how much I loved you then! I could say it and mean it but it wasn't like this, there wasn't all this—all this time between us, all the being there for each other, that's what started it for me, this whole fucking place has treated me like some fucking freak since—they want women in the Army sure they do! To cook and type and ball the men, but give them something different, let me break the fucking curve and I'm a freak, ol' Ballbuster Cole, they forget he came at me, those pukes would've let him kill me if I hadn't been able to stop him myself! Nikki doesn't exist except with you, Elen. The Old Man called me BB today, give me a break! You've never called me that, if it wasn't for you I wouldn't have an identity at all, I'd forget who I am and—don't, don't touch me Elen don't—" But she had, she did; Nikki collapsed as Elen drew her into her arms to hold her. "Elen I can't help it I love you—"

"Okay, Nikki. Shhhh . . . it's all right, Nikki. It's okay." Those calm and soothing murmurs of comfort; it took a long time, but they eased her, and still Elen held her, her hands tender against her back, smoothing her hair from her face, holding her head in the curve of her shoulder; even when they both knew the hurt was subsided, she held her, and when Nikki's lips brushed the smoothness of her throat Elen couldn't hide the shiver that rippled through her. "Nikki, I'm sorry," she whispered. "God, I never meant to hurt you—"

"You never did, Elen." As briefly and softly as she had kissed her the first time—the only time—she kissed her now: a controlled brush that found no response but regret before she broke gently from her arms. "You never hurt me, Elen. All you did was love me, and all I did was love you. It was all the same—and it was all just way too different."

Monday afternoon when Elen got home from work, Nikki Cole was gone.

CHAPTER FIVE

Elen, my love.

I wish I could have faced you but it would have killed me to say goodbye to you. I tried to imagine it and I couldn't get past the place where we said goodbye. I couldn't see us shaking hands, or just turning away. All I could see was that I'd have to kiss you. I know you'd have let me, but I knew you'd lose part of your love for me, for my weakness, and I wanted to leave knowing you love me. I know you do.

I told Major Dillinger I was gay. She said she didn't care. I told her if she didn't throw me out I'd tell Cheeseballs; at least she could let me go with some dignity. She saw that. She's a good person, Elen, and she has a lot of respect for you. (She sent Hogle to Korea.) I gave her my brother's address and phone number in Boston and asked her to give it to you if you want it; you can reach me through him. Maybe we can have a beer sometime when you're in town, if you're ever in town.

I still can't say goodbye, Elen. I can only say I love you. I wish I had been strong enough just to be your friend. — Nikki

❏   ❏   ❏

"McNally! Phone!" the Charge of Quarters bawled Tuesday morning as she was fumbling with shirt buttons, and she answered to the Executive Officer ordering her presence at the head shed, never mind formation, she was accounted for and if Chuckie Cheeseballs didn't like that he could damn well direct his complaints to the XO. Elen didn't feel like laughing; she had spent the night staring at Nikki's empty bed

48

and the maple bookcase she had left behind, reading her letter over and over again, but the major calling the lieutenant by his nickname made her laugh. "On the double, McNally," Dillinger snapped, and Elen swallowed the laugh and wondered what in hell she had done to incur the wrath of the Executive Officer. If there was a bad side in the battalion not to be on, it was Major Kare Dillinger's, West Point nagging or not. She met her section sergeant at the door and told him she wouldn't be present for morning formation, and went, jumpy-stomached, to salute the woman. "Private First Class McNally reports as requested, ma'am."

"At ease," the major said, a concession however brusquely stated. "Jesus, McNally, you look like you just lost your best friend."

You know I did! Why are you fucking with me? She reined in the flare; to growl at NCOs and shavetail lieutenants was thinkable. Snarling at Dillinger was a one-way ticket to a slick sleeve, and that PFC brass was brand-new. "I did," she said stiffly. "Ma'am."

"I know you did," the major said quietly. "And I'm sorry, Elen. Sit." McNally looked warily at her. "Sit, Mac," the major said gently, and she waited for McNally to settle cautiously into the chair across her desk. "Smoke if you want to." The ashtray she offered was usually reserved for Colonel Buckman and the Sergeant Major, the only two people in the unit she had even nominal interest in appeasing; McNally smiled a taut thanks for the offer but didn't light up. "Elen, if there'd been any way to make her stay, I would have. But you know what Cheeseballs would've done with that tidbit of information she dropped on me, don't you?"

Soldiers in trouble were part of the Executive Officer's job. Nikki Cole had been desperate and determined and technically easy to deal with, but when she said "Take it easy

on Elen, will you? I'm not telling her I'm leaving, and she's
going to be so hurt," she had wrecked Kare Dillinger's day.
McNally was one of the best soldiers in the battalion, and the
major didn't want to see her self-destruct; the kid in her office
now looked as if she was one wrong word away from that.
"Take a few days off," she said quietly. "Go to San Antonio
and do the River Walk. Go to Galveston and play in the Gulf.
Go somewhere. Do something. Just get out of this godfor-
saken place and try to heal."

McNally looked at her in bewilderment; she raised a
silencing hand. "Be back Monday. Your leave won't be
charged; you're temporary duty, special assignment for me.
Bring me back some military history: a piece of the Alamo,
a lock of Jim Bowie's hair—something. But go. I know she
meant a lot to you."

She could see it connect: nagging Elen about West
Point, complimenting her on her writing, keeping people out
of her hair when she was burning up the keyboard on important work—that was simply leadership, and she knew Elen
accepted it as such. This was above and beyond, and they both
knew it. Smoky hazel eyes showed understanding, relief—
and a raw flare of minds meeting. Kare knew they would
never again be simply Major and Private. Somewhere in their
undercurrents, they would be friends.

"Means," Elen corrected quietly. "We weren't lovers,
Major Dillinger, but she's not past tense yet."

"I know you weren't. She said you weren't and I believe
that. And I know she isn't past tense. I know she won't be for
a long time. I lost a friend not too long ago," she said softly;
Rachel had been more than just a friend, and her death a year
ago was a still-healing scar. "I remember, Elen. I remember
feeling like my heart had just been ripped out my throat. I
remember how badly I needed some time to lick my wounds.

No one gave it to me, but I can give it to you. Now go, before formation breaks. And don't get lost, squirt; you're a damned good troop and I want you back, or I wouldn't be doing this."

It was a moment before Elen knew the tears would hold; when she was sure, she stood. "I knew you were an exception, but I didn't expect this," she whispered. "Thank you." She hesitated. "And getting your heart yanked out your throat is just how it feels. I'm sorry about your friend, Major Dillinger."

Kare saluted her. Elen returned it. It had been a while since either of them had done it with such respect.

❏   ❏   ❏

The piece of the Alamo was easy; she picked up a stone in the yard of that shrine and slipped it into her pocket. Jim Bowie's hair was harder. She went to four barbershops before finding a red-haired man in the chair, and had to tell the barber a complex lie about tying a trout fly named the Red-Headed Stranger in honor of Texas's own Willie Nelson before he'd let her have a lock of the hair on the floor. She whip-finished one end of it with silk thread (thinking that a strand of the major's long coppery hair would have made a better knot, but Major Dillinger didn't leave such pieces of herself in the women's room at battalion headquarters). She bought a shadow box, some fine silver wire, a piece of matte board. She lettered the board, and mounted the stone and the lock of hair in the shadow box with the wire. The chore took some six hours— six hours in which she didn't miss Nikki quite as hard as she would have without the diversion, even knowing how much she would have enjoyed the joke.

She wondered about Major Dillinger. In what Nikki called the good guy-bad guy game, the leggy auburn-haired woman played a hard-core bad guy to Buckman's easy-going good guy: everybody liked Bucky, but the XO, beautiful as she was, was a relentless, doper-busting bitch, feared by the line troops, given wide berth by the headquarters staff; even junior officers tiptoed around her. But it was Dillinger who nagged her unmercifully about West Point, Dillinger Nikki had gone to so that she might go with dignity, Dillinger who gave her time to recover from losing a friend—why? Yes, it felt like getting her heart pulled out her throat, but how had the major known the depth of feeling between them? How had she known if she offered a week off and a Boston address Elen would have been on the next plane out of Dallas/Fort Worth bound for Logan? Why had she sent Hogle to Korea? Why had she told Nikki that, that Nikki might tell her? Why—

Why did it hurt so much to think of Nikki, why did she look at that letter fifty times a day to read the words she knew by heart: *Elen, my love. I still can't say goodbye, I can only say I love you.* Why did she wish with a deep, hard ache that she'd just slipped onto the bed beside her to discover the way-difference, why was it so easy now to imagine them touching with sweet, slow intimacy when she hadn't been able to in time to save them both getting their hearts ripped out their throats? *Nikki, why did you go? God, if you'd just given me a little more time—*

❑   ❑   ❑

She didn't have to see into the room; she felt another presence as soon as she unlocked the door. She braced herself and found Jeannie Kincaid on Nikki's bed, looking like anywhere else would have been a better option. "It wasn't my idea, Mac. That dickhead Cheeseballs put me in here. He said you couldn't have a room to yourself."

Shakily, Elen smiled. "Thank god it's you, Jeannie. I couldn't even have dealt with anyone else. I'll do the laundry—ironing included—if you'll keep this place clean."

"Deal. I hate ironing."

"Not as much as I hate housework." She offered her hand. "Welcome to room one-oh-four, Jeannie. Nikki and I called it the Haven."

"I could use one. I've spent a year with Trapp and Iver." She accepted Elen's hand. "I know we never hung out, Mac, but I miss Nikki, too. She was like, this voice of sanity in this suckhole place? And there ain't anybody over to the mess hall can cook an omelet like hers."

"Yeah," Elen murmured. "She did make a mean omelet." Nikki Cole's famous one egg omelet—except she used two eggs. *Elen, my love. I still can't say goodbye; I can only say I love you.*

❏   ❏   ❏

Nikki:

Please keep in touch. I always want to know where I can find a friend if I need one. I want to know you can, too.

I'm ready for that beer. Only the best for the best?

No goodbyes, Nikki. Not for us; not ever. I love you, too—I wish I had been brave enough to be your lover. — Elen

She sealed it into an envelope and took it and a tiny fakery to Major Dillinger's office and tapped on the door. "Ma'am? I've got my temporary duty report for you?"

"I figured you thought that was a vacation," the major grumbled. "Let's have it, McNally. We don't need to bother the colonel with this; close that door." Elen nodded her apology for the intrusion to Colonel Buckman; he gave her a welcome-home smile as she swung the door between the offices closed. "So how did you find San Antone?" *How's your heart?* the green eyes asked.

"I just took I-35 south, ma'am. There it was." *Healing. Thank you for the time.* "I hope you don't mind the lack of a written report, ma'am. Given your instructions, I guessed this would suffice."

Buckman smiled at the laugh that came from Dillinger's office, suspecting there might be a beer at the Officers' Club over this one. There would be, but he would not be shown the words Elen had dared put on the backing of the frame:

You are rare indeed. You'll always be special to me. Thank you for helping me get my heart back where it belongs . . . and if you're ever in Maine and need a drink, call me. I'll buy. Yours: Elen.

She had laughed at the contents of the shadowbox, but the words on the back stung unexpected tears to her eyes; they were both discomfited by how long it took her to recover. "I'm glad I could help," she managed, at last.

"You did. A lot." She looked at the envelopes in her hand. "If I could ask one more thing—"

The major raised an eyebrow.

"Nikki said she gave you a forwarding address. If you'd write it twice, ma'am? Once on this—" She gave the major a sealed, stamped envelope with only Nikki's name in her own neat, assertive printing. "And once to put in this." Another envelope, addressed and stamped, but open and empty. "Seal it and mail them if you would, ma'am?"

On the flap of the empty envelope was printed, "Dad please just put this in your safe." Dillinger read that, and she tapped the envelope against her desk before she looked up. "What did you learn in San Antonio, Elen?"

Elen hesitated, but the dark green eyes were steady, unguarded; she felt the undercurrent of friendship and knew honesty now could only strengthen it. "That gaining someone I know I can respect makes up for some of the losing someone I didn't dare to love," she said at last. "And . . . carpe diem."

For a moment she felt searched by those intense eyes; she allowed it, and at last Dillinger gave her a tiny, unreadable smile and opened her top desk drawer. "I'll mail your letters, Elen. I guess that's not too much to ask, given a piece of the Alamo and a lock of Jim Bowie's hair."

Even from her distance, Elen recognized the smooth, slanted script on the slip of paper the major drew from her desk. "I never expected you when I joined the Army, Major Dillinger," she said softly.

Again, those eyes: unwavering, penetrating. "I don't think the Army quite expected you either, Elen McNally."

❏   ❏   ❏

"Any mail for me, Hank?"

Henry Cole looked up from his before-dinner gin and tonic to study his baby sister. She had always been slender; she had been thin when she had come home from Texas. In the two weeks she'd been home, she had grown gaunt. "Not today, sweetie. Sorry," he said, and Nikki turned; the disappointment on her face was almost physical. "Honey," he said softly, "if she cared, she'd have written by now, don't you think?"

"She cared."

Henry watched her leave his den. He tasted his gin. When he finished his drink, he ensured his desk was locked. In the center drawer was an envelope with a Texas postmark, and one addressed to Texas, its stamp uncancelled.

It was bad enough that Nikki was queer. She didn't have to convert people, and while she was under his roof, Henry Cole would have no part of her trying.

❑   ❑   ❑

"Daddy? That letter I asked you to hold in your safe? There should be an address and phone number in it. Would you give them to me?" Some remote part of her listened to her mother, but her breath was shallow in her while she waited, and she copied down what he said. "Thanks, Dad. I should be home the eighteenth unless I get held up in Boston." She ached for Maine, for her family; more than that, she ached for Nikki, and had for three months. She slipped a dime into the phone and dialed the number Major Dillinger had written down back in September and mailed home for her. *Maybe we can have a beer sometime when you're in town, if you're ever in town—*

"Yes, I'm looking for Nikki Cole?"

A brief silence, then a cautious male voice. "Who's calling?"

"Elen McNally."

A longer silence. "I'm sorry. I don't think you have the right number."

"But—please, give her a message? Tell her I'll be in Bos—" But she was talking to a dial tone. The operator asked her to deposit ninety cents. "Let that Christmas-spirited asshole pay it," she snarled, and jammed the phone into its cradle and spent the rest of the night wavering between being glad Jeannie was on her way home for Christmas leave and wishing she was still there in the Haven to talk to. *Elen, my love—* Mostly, she tried not to cry.

❑   ❑   ❑

She had a six-hour layover at Logan; she caught a cab and gave the address Major Dillinger had sent her father, borrowing Nikki's Boston accent so she wouldn't get driven all over hell and gone by the cabbie. She had him wait, and rang the bell of a handsome Cambridge home. "Nikki Cole, please," she said to a man who looked so much like Nikki it was eerie.

"I'm sorry," he said coolly. "You have the wrong address."

She looked him in his handsome big brown Nikki eyes. "Tell her the beer's still cold, Mr. Cole," she said softly. "Please tell her I'm still her friend, and my flight doesn't leave Logan until five. Bar Harbor Air."

Bar Harbor flight 143 lifted off at three minutes after five for Portland, Bangor and Presque Isle. Elen McNally was on it.

BOOK TWO: ELEN

CHAPTER SIX

"Thank you, Jesus," Elen murmured, finding the weight room of the gym empty at eight on a Friday night; Tuesday she'd had to put up with three guys more interested in giving her a ration of shit than in working out themselves. The scales had told her a month ago she had gained four pounds over Christmas; "You worry about four pounds?" the plump Jeannie Kincaid asked in disbelief.

Thinly, Elen smiled. "I went from one-twenty to two hundred a pound at a time."

The four pounds were long gone, and six more with them, but it felt good to work out again, and when she was flat on her back with a weight more than equal to her own balanced on a bar over her throat she didn't think about Nikki Cole or the letters she wrote that were never answered; she thought about keeping a hundred and forty pounds from overpowering her and squashing her like a bug. Rules were no bench presses without a spotter, but no one had come in by the time she was ready for them. There were guys out in the gym playing pickup bucketball; if she yelled loud enough, they'd hear. It didn't escape her that yelling with a hundred and forty pounds crushing her throat would only be a neat trick if she could do it.

She settled onto the bench and was apexing her fifth press when the door opened. "Spot, please," she gasped with the bar on her chest, and sent it up again knowing no other lifter would refuse the request.

Ten. She listened to her breath, watching the insides of her eyelids; it was coming harder. Maybe fifteen was a little enthusiastic with so much weight. *Eleven.* Her biceps were starting to quiver; her pecs had been burning hard at nine. She gathered a breath and whooshed it out as she powered the bar up and—

Fuck! The cramp slammed hard and high into her left breast, a searing roar of pain that sucked the strength from her and her arms collapsed and there was no time and no way to get them back; she felt the bar hit her throat *Mama I love you* and knew she was—

"Let go of the bar."

The voice was calm and familiar and too far away to trust; she only knew she could breathe but it hurt and a lunatic cramp was raving deep in her left pec and if she let go of the bar it would kill her.

"Elen, let go of the bar. I've got it."

Whoever you are please don't be a lie— She opened nerveless fingers and the weight went away *oh goddess thank you* and the groan for the cramp came; she reached for it as the bar clanged to the brace. "You stupid shit! I ought to slap an Article Fifteen on you for wanton disregard for government property— which you are, McNally, and don't you ever forget it. Move your hand." Pain-fogged, still unsure of whose they were, she stood the fingers that walked the top of her pectoral until they found the knotted cramp; she sucked in an agonized breath. "Sorry. This only works when someone else does it." The heel of a hand pressured hard there, and a second wash of cold sweat prickled over her *don't puke this is—Jesus don't puke* and the knot loosened; she gasped, and the hand eased its pressure for knowing the pain had just become tolerable.

She sucked four huge breaths and finally dared look at her benefactor, finding deep green eyes and burnished-copper hair and a look that said the threat of the Article Fifteen was only that.

"You're dumber than a box of rocks, Mac." Major Dillinger went to one knee beside the bench, using her own towel to wipe sweat and tears from her face and neck. "I'm sorry I let you get bumped. I didn't expect that much weight. You okay?"

"Nnngh." It was the only response she could find. The major's hand at her throat was cool in a belated exploration of possible injury. She tried to remember if she'd ever been so terrified, and decided not. *Or so embarrassed. Why did it have to be her?* But grace was due; "thank you," she whispered.

"Anytime. Your mother would love knowing your last words were for her—and you're not required to call me Goddess until I make general." The major looked at the bar, adding up the plates. "A hundred and forty—Elen, are you out of your mind? How many past the burn did you go?"

"Three." It came out raspy; her throat had felt a much harder bump than she had really taken. She struggled to sit up, getting some help from an arm around her shoulders. "And yes, I know better. Please don't yell at me."

Long-nailed fingers caught her chin; startled, she met the dark green eyes. "You don't know for shit!" Dillinger almost spat it, but her eyes didn't match the hardness in her voice. "Don't you know what the burn is? It's muscle fiber self-destructing from overwork. Go past it like that and you'll

hurt yourself bad. I ought to bust you anyway, for working
without a spotter. Jesus, Elen, you could have died."

Those fingers at her jaw rode a thin edge between
getting her attention and hurting; she reached for the major's
wrist. "Please let go of me—" It was all the warning she could
give.

She didn't let go, but she backed off her grip to something very close to gentle, something very briefly almost a
caress. "I'm sorry," she said softly. "I was scared too, Elen."
Her touch trailed away. "Go get an ice pack from the deep-
freeze, Squirt, and keep it there for twenty minutes, and get
another one and do it again. Maybe by then you'll have
enough starch to spot for me." She stood, and pulled Elen up
by the right hand and gave her a send-off swat on the ass.
"You come back with that ice," she ordered, hard-core again,
"or Monday morning I'll lock your heels so hard you'll think
somebody welded your boots together. I'm not done with you
yet."

❏   ❏   ❏

Too stupid by Major Dillinger's assessment to be allowed to work out alone, Tuesday and Friday nights Elen met
the major at the gym. The guys pretty much left them alone,
most ignoring them, some teasing gently enough that neither
of them took offense, a few offering good advice, but the hair
on the back of Elen's neck rose one Friday night when a tall
and heavy-muscled sergeant came in, glowering when he saw
them. He bulled across the room as if he had to force aside
the air.

Dillinger was doing high-rep, low-weight bench
presses, Elen spotting for her. They had been alone until him.
"Trouble," Elen murmured. "Bigtime."

The brawny sergeant kicked a booted foot against the end of the bench. "Unass it, cunt," he growled. "You don't belong here."

Dillinger opened her fingers. Elen racked the bar. Goddess-beautiful, rock-hard, the major rose to her full five-foot-eleven, her smile as cold and dangerous as spring ice. The sergeant took a step back, not as certain as he had been. She offered her ID card for his perusal. He saw blue ink that meant officer and read the rank and paled, as she said with terrible gentleness, "You have the right to remain silent. Anything you say can, and will, be used against you. Anything you want to add, hot shot?" He had nothing to add. (What he would have would be fifteen days in the stockade to consider the phrase gross insubordination, and he would emerge with far fewer stripes and far less pay than he'd had going in.)

"Goddamned men," the major muttered when the MPs had taken him away; she stood fists on hips in the middle of the weight room, disgusted, angry, more shaken than she cared to admit; had Elen been alone here, had he done and said to Elen what he'd done and said to her, she knew that Elen, without the weight of a blue ID card to fall back on, and with that unpredictable temper of hers, would probably have gotten herself hurt. She turned to see Elen sitting on a bench, her elbows on her knees and an unreadable look in her smoky hazel eyes. "What," she almost snapped.

Elen stood. "Maybe I shouldn't say this—"

"Then don't."

"—but I think you're great. You're an incredibly powerful woman. You're the best officer I could even imagine. I've never met anyone, in the Army or anywhere, that I respect any more than I do you, Major Dillinger. If I take any pride in being a soldier, I take it from serving with you."

She was almost to the showers before the major found her voice. "Elen!"

She turned.

"Thank you," the major said softly. "Thank you very much."

❑   ❑   ❑

Jeannie Kincaid hit the ninety-day loss list in February, and Elen counted the days down with her, dreading losing her as a roommate. She wasn't Nikki; no one was Nikki, but she was a good roomie. Chuckie Cheeseballs was ahead of her on the loss roster; by order of the commander and over Gouda's howl of protest, Elen bore the guidon in his change of command ceremony. It had been the lieutenant's bad judgment to tell her when she came eligible for promotion to Specialist Fourth Class that he had truckers in his motor pool he'd promote whether they deserved it or not before he'd promote a goddamned WAC working out of her MOS. At the gym, she repeated the conversation to Dillinger, and the major pinned the new rank on her collar herself shortly after writing Chuck a less than glowing Officer Evaluation Report that she had Elen type.

"God, Boss," she mourned one Friday over a beer at the Officers' Club, where the major took her sometimes when they left the gym; their friendship was a puzzling blend of cautious warmth and strict formality, and she hadn't been invited to first-name basis. "I hate to think of breaking in a new roomie when Jeannie gets out. She's way short."

A day before Jeannie left, the major pinned acting sergeant's stripes on Elen, for NCOs were entitled to private quarters. But when Rae Vitale, thirty-five and brassy, busted down from sergeant for the third time in a ten-year hitch, came to the unit, Elen watched her brutal ostracism by Trapp and

Iver, into whose room she had been put; she saw Vitale's confidence fade day by day to hurt bewilderment as they wore her down. She invited Rae into her room for a beer. "I'll do the laundry—including ironing—if you'll keep this damn room clean." And Rae of the rose tattoo between her breasts became Elen McNally's third roommate.

Rae didn't care to read, and had been too recently reminded of how much trouble she could get into when she partied; the tattoo was but one instance of proof. She kept the room immaculate, and shined Elen's brass and boots along with her own because she was good at it and it gave her something to do. Her humor was ribald, her sense of justice more biblical than poetic, her interest in philosophical discussion nonexistent, but she was kindhearted and generous, and Elen liked her because of that, and respected her crude intelligence and canny knowledge of how to get along within the system—as long as she wasn't halfway to the worm in a fifth of Mexico's finest high-octane cactus juice. They settled easily into each others' lives.

❏   ❏   ❏

Elen's second Texas summer wandered along, uneventful. The Deuce had its annual general inspection and passed with an overall commendable, an almost unheard-of feat; at the unit party she tried to keep Rae out of the beer with success that was limited but enough to keep Rae from deciding to take a pop at some NCO or officer, which was how she'd gotten busted the last time.

She woke up blackly depressed one day and knew why when she remembered the date; one year ago today, Nikki had left. "Ahhh, shit—" She sat on the edge of her bed to run her hands through her hair and stare out the window. "McNally, you need therapy. You really do."

For a year she had written, and got nothing back; she still wrote. She called, and Henry snarled at her to leave him and his sister alone. She went to work every day, worked out with the major twice a week, kept Rae sober on weekends, and it was all just something to keep her mind off what it always went back to when there was nothing to distract it. She missed Nikki with an ache like the phantom pain of a missing limb.

She dragged through a slow day, wishing there was more for her to do. At four Major Dillinger caught her with her feet on her desk, arms and ankles crossed, glowering at the back wall of her tiny office and trying not to cry. "God, Squirt. You look like ten miles of bad road."

"I feel like twenty. Let's go."

The gym was empty; the weight room was theirs. Elen pulled cast-iron plates from a bar, clanging them to the floor, griping under her breath— "Sons a whores, every bar in the place loaded to the fuckin gunnels, they could have some friggin courtesy" —until a hand settled onto her shoulder; she jerked her head around in near-resentment. "What!"

"Why don't you tell me what's wrong," the major said quietly.

She ducked her head away from the gentle green eyes. "It's personal."

"That doesn't mean you've got to let it eat you alive, Mac."

Elen secured the collar on one end of the bar and moved to the other.

"Elen, I won't let you work like this. You'll hurt yourself. Can't you talk to me?"

"Jesus!" It exploded from her, punctuated by a sidearmed fling of a collar into a corner; cast iron met cinderblock in echoing impact. "Look, I feel like an idiot, all right?

So you want me to tell you so you'll know I'm one? Can you just lay off me? Please?"

And she knew by the quick, startled look in Major Dillinger's eyes that she had hurt her, but she couldn't find the breath to apologize as the major studied her in long silence before turning away. "Sorry," Dillinger said, carefully neutral. "I thought I could help. I guess I can't."

"Oh, shit—" She scrambled to her feet and followed her into the locker room. "I'm sorry. Please, Ka—Major Dillinger, I'm—"

"Don't worry about it." The major shucked her fatigue shirt and hung it in her locker, and sat to loosen her boots. "I was prying."

"You were trying to be a friend, and I'm being a jerk. It's a year today since Nikki left, and it still hurts and I feel stupid and I don't know how to handle it, but I was wrong to unload on you and I'm sorry. I really am. I never meant to hurt your feelings."

The major didn't look up from unlacing her boots; Elen didn't know if she was angry or hurt or both. Knowing she was crossing an intricate, precarious line, not knowing what else to do, she touched hesitant fingertips to the officer's shoulder. "Major Dillinger, I'm sorry," she said softly. "Please. I don't know what else to say."

"Then it must be my turn." The major stood, and Elen almost flinched from her sinuous height, certain that now she would be dismissed from this strange friendship she knew she had gotten too comfortable in. Buck sergeants didn't snarl at majors. They surely never assumed the ability to wound, and only a fool would have iced an already imprudent cake with the audacity of a personal touch. She clamped her teeth and jammed back the tears and forced herself to meet the major's eyes, expecting nothing more or less than *I'll see you in my*

office Monday morning; have your brass in your hand.
"Ma'am—"

And her knees almost buckled when the major took her face in both hands and touched her lips to her forehead, her voice gentle: "Elen, it's all right." The tears she had been crowding back all day defeated her last effort to hold them. When the major smoothed the first one away, she was too far away from the last tenderness given her, too far from Nikki; she broke. "Come here," Major Dillinger whispered. "God, honey, you need to cry—" and Elen went wounded into the safety of her arms and buried her face in the soft rise of her breast and let go. She cried for the loneliness, the emptiness, the uncertainty; she cried for homesickness and brief haven and the gentleness of a woman's touch at her back and her hair and her being; she cried for everything she missed.

"I don't even know who I am," she whispered at last, retreating from the sanctuary of the major's warmth, embarrassed by having needed it, confused by it having been offered. "I—thank you."

A hand squeezed her shoulder. "'S'okay. Can you talk now? Do you want to?"

"I—" She leaned wearily against the lockers, her back to the major. "God, this is so hard," she said softly. "It's hard to even think about. I just don't think it's something you'd really understand. I mean—"

"I might surprise you, Mac."

Elen reeled off a wad of toilet paper and blew and wiped and sniffed a breath of bald courage. "I wasn't gay when she left, and that's why she left. But that's how I miss her. I miss her as a friend, but I . . . I . . ."

The major waited; finally she said, "Would it be easier to talk to someone gay about it, Elen? Would they understand better?"

"I guess that's it. It's not that I—" Helplessly, she shrugged, staring at the floor. "Major Dillinger, I really like you. I trust you. And I respect your opinion more than anyone's, but—"

"But I'm straight?"

"Yeah."

"Wrong."

Cautiously, Elen looked up.

Major Dillinger shrugged, in concession, or confession. "I'm a lesbian. If that makes it any easier, if you still want to talk—"

Leaping past surprise—later, it would occur to her to be amazed, not so much that the officer was a lesbian, but that she would admit it to an enlisted person—she pounced on the question. "How did you know you were?"

The major leaned against the lockers with a small sigh. "Elen, I think almost every woman, sometime in her life, has a physical attraction to another woman. Some of us act on it. Some don't. Some of us accept it. Some don't. Some of us embrace it. I did."

Elen paced halfway to the showers, stopped, considered the memory of Kare Dillinger's arms around her, the feel and the scent and the warmth of her, and she turned. "I know I've got two basic questions, and I know they're related, but it's like the strings are too short to tie a knot. One is, am I gay, and the other one is, why can't I get past her, whether I am or I'm not?" She shook her head. "I feel like I just parachuted into a mine field," she said softly. "One wrong step and some question's going to blow up in my face." She ran a hand through her hair. "Like this one. Big potential to step on my figurative dick here. Here you are, this . . . this goddess-woman. We have a relationship of some sort. If I'm a lesbian, shouldn't I be attracted to you?"

"'Goddess-woman'?" The major's smile showed the compliment taken; Elen looked away shyly, surprised the words had slipped out. "Thank you, Elen. But to try to answer your question, are straight women turned on by every man just because he's a man? If Nikki's your type, chances are I'm not. And as far as our relationship goes—Elen, I think of you as a friend, and I wish we could be more open with it, but rumor control aside, you're a non-com and I'm a field-grade and I sign off on your evaluation. We can't be—"

"I know all that. That's not my question, Ka—" For the second time, she stumbled over, and caught back, the familiarity. "—Major."

"You can call me Kare here, Elen."

"Thank you—but it's not a good habit to get into, for the reasons you said." Her smile was drawn, tired. "I'll just call you Goddess and let people figure out if there's room to argue with me. Next question: How do I get to her? And if I can't, how do I get past her?"

Kare sat on the bench by the lockers. "Elen, maybe she was just supposed to be a catalyst in your life," she said quietly. "Maybe you and Nikki were never supposed to be. Maybe she had something to tell you, and it's up to you to find out if she was right." She rubbed at the back of her neck, and pulled the pins from her hair; it tumbled over her shoulders in a lush copper cascade, and Elen noticed it and categorized its beauty and felt nothing more than appreciation for that beauty, one more part of a woman lovely from so many angles. "And maybe it's time you thought about letting her go," the major said softly. "I can't tell you if you're gay or not. I can only say don't try to decide. Try to accept. If you're straight, you have to deal with the rape—"

Elen huffed a small, hurt laugh. "You knew about that."

"Yes. And if you're gay, you have to deal with that. Either way, you have to deal with Nikki. I wish I could tell you how."

"I wish you could, too," she almost whispered, and she sat there on the bench; at last she asked quietly, "Do you have someone? Someone who loves you?"

It was a long moment before the major answered. "There's someone I love. Why do you ask?"

"My mind's like an old roll-top desk. It gives me a pigeonhole to put you in." She stood, and started to unbutton her fatigue shirt, and stopped. "So do we work out, or do we find us some off-limits country-music roadhouse whar the jukebox plays weepin' steel guitar 'til closin' time?"

She was so drawlingly Texas she could have passed for native. The major gave her a weak grin. "An' whar th' two a.m. sport o' choice is bashin' faggot wimmin? Ah vote for workin' out, Squirt."

"Spot for me, then. I'm going for one-seventy-five. Eight of 'em."

"You're out of your mind."

"That's what you said the first time you saved my life, Goddess."

Kare watched her out the door. *Yes, Elen. Yes, there's someone I love.*

❏   ❏   ❏

West Fort Hood was the color of age, of dried things, of weariness and the fingers of old men who rolled their own smokes from a can. In August it was dry as a corpse, the air as stale as cigarettes found in the pocket of last year's coat, a treacherous, alien landscape brimming with sidewinders and scorpions and small biting things that sought folds of human skin to lay their eggs where they would itch and infect. The

Deuce went there in late August to be tested on its ability to survive; the troops pitched their tents and strung their razor wire and played their game of war, and three times a chopper landed: once for a heart attack, once for a man bitten crazy by the chiggers, once to pick up a body in a bag, and the Deuce returned to Main Post eight days later, older and wiser and fewer.

CHAPTER SEVEN

Bill Buckman took a photograph out at West Fort of his operations clerk and Executive Officer walking away from the command post together late in the sixth afternoon of their second field exercise in as many months. He snapped the picture quickly, meaning only for a memory of that good friendship; he got back a print he would later have enlarged and framed, and it would hang in his offices for years: Elen, tall, lean even in field gear, her helmet under one arm, early-October sunset glinting from her golden hair as she looked up at the even longer-legged officer; it was the angle of her head that caught his heart, the tilt that said 'I need your help . . .' and Kare's whole stance, the turn of her shoulders, the way her head was bent to listen, said 'if I can, I will.'

To Buckman, the picture exemplified what leadership could and should be; he saw an officer and an enlisted person in a moment of deep, mutual respect. It wouldn't have mattered had he known the subject of the conversation; he'd have thought no less of Elen had he heard her say, "How can I feel what I feel for Nikki and all of a sudden want another woman so bad I can't sleep nights? I feel like I'm going crazy, Goddess. Is this anything close to normal?"

I had to ask, Kare thought. She knew August and September had been hard on Elen, and for the last two weeks

75

she'd been wired; field duty again so soon was only stringing her tighter. "Come on," Kare had said five minutes earlier. "Why don't we do walkie-talkies before you come un- wound." *So now I know.* "There is no normal, Squirt, and even if there was, you wouldn't be it." She bummed a smoke from the pack Elen drew from a pocket and waited for the light. "I guess I've got some questions," she said quietly. "I don't need to hear the answers, but I'd like to think you knew them before you just charge off into something. Do you know this woman? Is she a friend? Did you meet her last week and she looks like Nikki so you're transferring? Are you tired of wondering if you are or you aren't and you're looking for a way to find out? Because if you're just curious—"

"It's not that." Elen scuffed at the ground with the toe of her boot. "And she doesn't look anything like Nikki. And I've known her a long time. It feels like I'm—I don't know. In love, or something. I'm so confused."

"You need to let go of Nikki or you'll only be using this other woman," Kare said gently, and Elen looked at her, a look impossible to decipher. "I know it's hard, Squirt. I know you're not getting a lot of help with it—"

The hazel eyes were smoky, heavy-lidded as always, but she had never seen this look in them before; it was intensely, almost uncomfortably personal. "I've got you, Kare," Elen said quietly. "That's major help, no pun in- tended."

The major shied her look away, out across the grizzled landscape, not seeing the rainwash gullies, the grazing range cattle, the dusty scrub cedar; all she saw was the look in Elen's eyes. *I've got you, Kare—*

Elen had never called her by her name before.

God, Elen, you do. If only you knew how you've got me.

She didn't know the words would escape her until they had. "Birds of a feather," she whispered; she met those eyes again, an almost physical impact. "God, Elen. Sometimes I—"

"Major Dillinger! Division on the horn, ma'am, the general wants you!"

"Jesus! He can want in one hand and shit in the other and see which one gets full first," Kare muttered, not knowing if the interruption had been a blessing or a curse; Elen was studying her, a cautious question deep in her eyes. "Sorry, Squirt," she said softly. "Duty calls."

"I'm off at midnight, if you've got time to talk."

"Who's got time for a life?" Kare went to answer the field phone, and at half-past midnight when Buckman ordered her to get some sleep she found Elen idling against a jeep outside the command post, smoking and watching the stars. Kare knocked on her helmet; Elen looked up with a lazy smile. "I thought you were off-duty, Sergeant." *God, don't look at me like that—*

"I am, Major, but I thought I'd risk my stripe and tell you I've got a jug of scotch in my crib that's so good it's cruel. Take the edge off the day?"

Kare hesitated only a moment. "I'll risk my little gold oak leaf and say how goddamned grateful I am that you do. I was ready yesterday." She followed Elen to a low thicket fifty yards behind the command post and laughed when Elen lifted a sweeping cedar bough, offering it as a door. "What great camo! I must come by twenty times a day and I didn't know there was a tent here."

"No one does, except Bucky and Guzman. Be it ever so humble, it's home, and it's private." She lit a candle and dug into her duffle bag, coming up with a fifth, giving Kare's canteen cup a liberal gurgle of Chivas before she poured for herself. "You started to say something earlier," Elen said; their fatigue shirts were off, their T-shirts sticking to them in heat that still simmered in the Texas night. "Sometimes, you said. Sometimes you something."

"Yeah. Sometimes I talk too much." Kare tasted her drink. Cross-legged in the tiny tent, their knees necessarily touched; she was painfully aware of the contact. "Did you hear Bucky tell about almost getting captured? That'd be a hell of a coup for the bad guys, taking a battalion commander prisoner."

"Better him than you, Goddess. They play hardball with female POWs here."

Kare heard the hard memory in Elen's voice: Rae Vitale had come home from August's field exercise in a zippered bag. Elen had found her body, and Kare knew she would never forget her eyes when she had come into the command post to interrupt Buckman as he briefed the division commander: Sir, I have a casualty report. Not now, Bill snapped, but Kare had stayed the irritated general with one hand on his shoulder, the colonel with her other; Report, Sergeant McNally, she said, and Elen did, into her eyes because they were the only safe place for her then, staccato as machine-gun fire: I found Private First Class Rae Vitale half a click north-northwest of this location, I posted a guard, she's dead, ma'am—and when the colonel and general had upended their chairs in their haste to confirm the casualty Kare and Elen had been momentarily alone in the command post, Kare knowing a jumble of things: how long Elen had been without sleep, how much she cared for her brassy, irritating roommate, how great the shock in her eyes.

And how deeply she loved Elen McNally. "Are you all right?" she had asked with soft intensity. "Elen, honey, tell me now. Are you all right?"

"No," Elen had said hollowly, and something visceral and gritty gathered in her; Kare watched it happen. "But I have to be, Goddess. Don't I."

Now, Kare touched the .45 at her hip; Buckman had ordered her to carry it with live rounds, and she hadn't protested. "Squirt, there is some shit up with which I will not put. Any little puppy that tried me would find his young ass rode hard and put away wet, and not like he had in mind."

"I guess I'd rather try to poke marshmallows up a wildcat's ass than try to talk you into something you didn't want to do." Elen's smile was something between a hard reminiscence and a right-now grin. "I know from dear experience your ability to bust a head."

Kare gave her a pained look. "Don't remind me. I figured I'd catch you with dilated pupils and make you piss in a jar. I was so embarrassed when you came out from under that truck bleeding like that, Elen."

"Hey. No harm, no foul." She looked away, and back; when she spoke, her voice had softened. "But don't look too close now if busting different kinds of heads is really your mission in life, Goddess. I had to get that way to dare to ask you over for a drink."

Kare met the hazel eyes over the candle flame. "There's a lot of blood under the bridge, Elen, for you to be needing Dutch courage all of a sudden."

Elen rocked her canteen cup slowly, watching the pale liquid slosh. "Birds of a feather," she said quietly. "I've been wondering what you meant, Kare. What you would have said if the general had given you time."

Maybe after another drink or four she'd be ready for that; she meant only to have one. "Elen, don't ever be stoned on duty. I won't have any choice."

"Yeah, Goddess." Faint, barely-there irony. "The Army gets better every time a doper gets busted. Does PJ score your smoke for you, too?"

Kare tasted her drink. She smoked, but not much. The only safe way for an officer to smoke dope was alone, and alone wasn't ever what she wanted to be when she was stoned; it made her liquidly horny, and being horny and alone was —well, being horny alone. It wasn't that it was no fun; it simply wasn't as much fun as the alternative . . . or nearly as dangerous, when the alternative was enlisted. "I'm on the fast track, Elen," she said gently. "There might be a star or two in my future. I can't see pissing that away for a buzz."

Elen's smile said the lack of a definitive no had been answer enough; she leaned indolently against her duffle, her T-shirt drawing snug across her hard-toned body. "You're my best buddy. Did you ever know I smoked?"

"You surprise me," Kare admitted. "I thought you were squeaky-clean."

"Sneaky-clean. Will you get high with me sometime?"

The look in those heavy-lidded hazel eyes caught the no back on her lips. How many times had she looked into those eyes, that she had never noticed how they were flecked with gold? Elen's knee pressured warmly against hers. "I'd love to." *Oh god that slipped out—Crazy! Jesus, it makes you so wet and you know how much you want her—*

From somewhere, Elen produced a slim, tightly-rolled joint. "You've seen the operations orders. Nothing going down tonight."

Kare looked at the joint, and at Elen; steadily, Elen held her look. "You can smoke with me, say no, or bust me," she said gently. "You know how I feel about you, Kare. There isn't enough money in Texas to buy me betraying you."

*I know how you feel about me? God, Elen, if only I knew!
Do you have a clue of how I feel about you?* She ran a hand
through her hair, and drew a breath and let it out softly. "So
fire it up." *You're nuts. Don't do this—*

Elen raised an eyebrow, a last chance out; she nodded,
and Elen leaned into the candle, taking the paper hit, and
offered the joint. Kare drew a deep breath and knew she was
crazy, and accepted it. She drew smoke deep and held it; it
was smooth and mellow. Elen's fingers were warm against
hers, taking it back. "You want a shotgun?"

God, those eyes—! "What's a shotgun?"

"Neophyte. It's the kiss of enlightenment." Elen shaped
the cherry of the joint. "I blow." Her eyes laughed gently.
"And you, Goddess—you suck." She put the hot end into her
mouth and Kare understood; she leaned to accept the smoke,
trying to ignore how nearly like a kiss this felt, trying not to
feel Elen's balancing fingertips lightly against her knee. The
first hit was spreading warm and deep in her; she opened her
eyes and was jolted by Elen's there to meet hers, and when
Elen's lips grazed her own, whether by accident or design,
that warmth blossomed into a fuller, deeper heat. "Enough,"
she whispered. *And too much. Get out of here; god, get out
of here—*

Elen picked the joint from her mouth just as a seed
exploded; they both jumped. "Nick of time. I thought I
cleaned this." Her voice was soft, full, throaty; Kare tried to
blame dope and whiskey, and not a brush of lips that had
surely been only an accident of nearness, as Elen took a last
toke and pinched out the joint. "You don't need much of this."

I can't take much of this.

"I don't like to get wasted. Just . . . focused."

I'm focused, all right. God, how I want you.

"What did you start to say this afternoon? Sometimes I wish—?"

"You're not going to leave that alone, are you."

"No. It felt important. Sometimes you what?"

Kare tasted her drink. The scotch was liquid heat, a match to a much more personal liquidity. "Drop it, Elen," she almost whispered. "Please."

"West Point to you too." Hazel eyes considered her for a long moment; she wanted to look away and couldn't. "Tell me, Kare," Elen said softly. That voice slipped around her name like a caress.

Kare closed her eyes, a soft breath escaping her; she knew when she opened them again those hazel eyes would be there. They were. "Damn you, Elen—" She wet her finger and thumb with her tongue and pinched out the candle. "Carpe diem, then." Her voice was as husky as Elen's had been. "Sometimes I wish—"

She reached across the darkness, her fingertips finding the sweat-dampness of Elen's throat. "Sometimes I wish you could look past Nikki far enough to see me." She let her fingers trace the line of Elen's jaw, her ear, through the damp thickness of her hair to the back of her neck. "Who keeps you up nights, Elen?" Softly, she asked; Elen's skin was slick and wet under her touch. "I wish it was me. God, I wish it was me."

Elen was suddenly there, close, catching Kare's face in her hands; there was only a breath between them. "God, Kare—" Her voice was raggedly intense. "Kare, don't you know it's you? Don't you know how much I want you?"

"Then take me—" It was all she had time to say before Elen's lips stopped her, a whiskey-spiced tongue probing deeply into her mouth, and fire exploded in her belly; she had wanted Elen McNally since the day she had come back from

San Antonio. Aching with desire, terrified of it, she had gotten stoned that night, and the fantasy had been long and slow and agonizingly detailed, her orgasm almost frightening in its intensity, and every Friday night since then had been an effort not to say come home with me—but now *at last—oh god, at last*—there was the reality of that tongue in her mouth, those hands buried in her hair, that belly hard against her breasts; she sought skin under Elen's shirt, raked her nails across the sleek muscularity of her back, answered her kiss with an urgency pent in her for more than a year. "Elen, come on—"

She gasped as Elen's knee pressed hard between her legs, one hand coaxing her T-shirt from its tuck, the other in her hair keeping her in a kiss that was beyond anything in her experience: that tongue flickering under her own had her riding the thin edge of orgasm. "Elen—oh, god! Come on—" She knew her need and her wetness as Elen's hands relieved her of her shirt; it flickered through her mind that neither of them had had more than a whore's bath for six days. She smelled their hot ripeness and knew it didn't matter as fingers found the button and then the zipper of her pants; when those fingers slipped under silk to part her soft, wet curls with barely-controlled desire, nothing mattered. She arched against that seeking hand, unable to stifle the hard moan when lips found the erection of her nipple. "Elen—god Elen please—" She locked her fingers in the thickness of Elen's hair, holding her head against her breast, her breath ripping from her. "Elen, be inside me, take me, do it now—" and when Elen closed gentle teeth on her nipple and probed two fingers deeply into her, Kare couldn't hold back; she could only hope she wouldn't scream as the molten explosion took her, a curling, heaving wave that reared and bucked and plunged her into a whirlpooling sea. She surfaced gasping, clinging to the raft that was Elen until the shudder ebbed and she could find a ragged, panting breath. "Elen—oh my god," she moaned, as those fingers slipped inside her again. "Elen, wait— god, I've never—god, never like that, Elen. God, how I've wanted you—"

"Do you want to rest?" Elen bore her gently to her back, a finger stroking slowly through the wet warmth of her, finding the swollen bud of her desire, a touch that sucked the breath from her again. "Should I stop?"

"God, no. Please—oh, god, please don't stop—"

Elen found her lips, whispering against them. "God, how you feel—I've never made love to a woman before, Kare. Teach me. Tell me what you want."

"Easy this time—slow—Elen, there—oh, honey, right there—you know how, Elen oh my god Elen kiss me don't let me scream—"

But much later, when she reached for the button of Elen's fly, that slim hand stopped her. "It's all right, Kare. I'm okay."

"Elen, please." She raised onto one elbow, leaning over her, tasting herself on Elen's lips. "I want you to come, too."

"I did."

Kare felt the smile against her lips.

"With you, Goddess. What a rush." Gently, she pulled Kare down to her, holding her. "I wish you could stay with me," she said softly. "I wish I could hold you while you sleep."

"We'd both be civilians by Friday," Kare murmured, tempted anyway by the tenderness of the arms around her; she may have been Elen's first woman, but Elen obviously knew what pleased her own body, and how to translate it. She had been just rough enough the first time with her hand, exquisitely gentle the last with her mouth; the only problem was that Kare was curled naked against a woman still fully clothed. Elen had undressed her with sensual indulgence, but hadn't even gotten out of her own T-shirt. Kare found the hem of that shirt and slipped her hand under it, smoothing her palm up that lean belly, brushing her fingertips across a soft nipple, feeling it crown under her touch. "Let me do for you what you did for me," she whispered. "I don't want to be selfish—"

"Oh, Kare, no." Elen spilled her onto her back, burying a deep, wanting kiss into her throat. "How can you think you were selfish? You gave yourself to me, Kare. You trusted me—you risked yourself for me. All I want is to do it again with light—I hated not being able to see you. God, you're so beautiful. If I could have seen your face when you were coming."

"You're shameless, Elen McNally," Kare laughed softly. "God, you are. If I told you I love you, would you hate it?"

"No. I was afraid to say it. I didn't think you'd believe me."

Gently, Kare kissed her. "I wouldn't have," she said quietly. "But your wanting me is one hell of a compliment, Elen. I'm old enough to be—"

"My big sister."

"Right, Squirt. With a kid your age."

"If I'd told you yesterday that I love you, would you have believed me? Could you have believed it from me as a friend?"

Kare studied the darkness where Elen was, feeling her above her, a calm, honest presence. "Yes," she said softly. "Yes, Elen, I could have. Now flick your Bic and help me find my clothes. I can't stay here all night."

"Is that an order, Major?"

"Yes it is, Sergeant—and for god's sake, make sure I get the shirt with the oak leaves on the collar."

❏   ❏   ❏

"Did I hear you say you know how to hang wallpaper?" Major Dillinger asked Sergeant McNally two days later, the unit back to some semblance of normalcy in garrison; Elen had just given Captain Guzman detailed instruction on how to cut a lapped seam. "I've got a dining room that needs it badly. Five bucks an hour for good help, if you've got some free time over the weekend."

Elen glanced at her. "Sorry. I'm going to Fort Worth this weekend."

"I thought you might like to pick up some extra dollars."

"I would, but Grateful Dead at the Convention Center sounds like a whole lot more fun than hanging paper, no offense, and I've got the ticket."

"Well, pardon me all to hell." The major was clearly irritated. "I need those enlisted evaluation reports sometime in this reign of Christ, McNally."

"Yes, ma'am." She hit the title with delicate derision.

The major aimed a finger at her. "Don't push your luck, Sergeant. Your evaluation isn't signed yet." She about-faced and stalked to her office.

"Jesus, Mac, I thought you two were buddies," Captain Guzman wondered at her. "What the hell was that all about?"

"Majors and sergeants aren't buddies. Yeah, we train together, but that doesn't mean I've got to give up my weekends."

"Maybe so, but just remember that her bad side is a hard place to be."

That camouflage out of the way, Elen spent the weekend at Kare's house, arriving on Friday night bearing twelve-year-old scotch and two slim joints of the same mellow dope they had shared out in the field. They smoked most of one; Kare cooked lobster and artichokes. They made sensuously indulgent, buttery messes of each other and got only as far as the living room before Elen took her to the floor, her hands and her mouth seeking what they both wanted, and in the privacy of her house on the far outskirts of Harker Heights, Kare didn't have to tell Elen not to let her scream when Elen's fingers and then her tongue found the depth of her desires. But when she was spent on the floor, her clothes scattered all over and Elen roaming small, teasing kisses across her nakedness, Elen was still clothed. "Is this some power thing?" she whispered, when Elen gentled her hand away from the buttons of her fly. "Are you trying to get back at me for outranking you? Elen, let me touch you. Please."

Elen didn't answer, and Kare couldn't argue when that delicate, pointed tongue did what it did in lieu of talking. When she awoke in the lightening early morning Elen was curled around her in her bed, holding her with her arms and legs, both of them smoothly naked, but when she slipped her hand up Elen's thigh and around she found herself suddenly on her back, her hands restrained above her head as Elen kissed her with a thoroughness that finally made her beg to be taken as Elen had taken her the first time; the difference now was the light. It was shimmeringly arousing to know those eyes were consuming her, both her wrists caught in one long-fingered hand while the other barely stayed on the gentle side of roughness between her thighs.

And even though she was taller and stronger and could have insisted, she knew it wouldn't have been the same; the difference was in the willingness, and Elen was once hurt. When Elen whispered, "Kare, please don't," she let it go, but she couldn't quite believe the drowsy whisper as they faded into sleep: *I love you.*

CHAPTER EIGHT

As operations clerk, Elen was first to see orders that came through the battalion, those pieces of paper that shuffled personnel from one place to another. They arrived Tuesdays from division headquarters, and she sorted them and kept the loss roster updated; it was just Tuesday afternoon to her.

"Orders," Specialist Carson said, back from the distribution run, flipping the big manila envelope onto her desk. "This is classified; sign here." She wrote her name for a blue-edged folder. "You sign for secret too?"

She wrote her name. She took the classified and secret folders to Captain Guzman and wiped down the loss roster board. It had three columns: ninety-, sixty-, and thirty-day losses, listed by rank. She pulled the batch of orders from their envelope and started sorting by grade: Enlisted/junior. Enlisted/senior. Officer/company grade. And a space on her desk for the possibility of officer/field grade. There were only Kare and Bill who would go to that space.

LOGAN, Jody W. 004-00-3759. SP4. 64C30. Fort Devens.

CHRISTOPHER, Allyn P. 826-32-3505. SSG. 71L30. Fort Lewis.

DILLINGER, Kare (NMI). 931-84-8174. MAJ. QMC. Heidelberg, Germany.

❏   ❏   ❏

"Lou, I'm asking for one lousy year. Give me a break, guy," Kare pleaded with the personnel officer at Department of the Army; Thursday, he'd cut her request for extension off before she could finish it. "The market sucks. I'll be stuck with this house for months. Have a heart, Lou. Don't make me a Fort Hood landlord."

"I appreciate your problem, but I can't extend you, honey. Somebody's got plans for you that don't include another year in the left armpit of the Army. You've got cut orders. Gomen na'sai, Major-san."

Kare thought Lou had been a bit of a pain in the ass since his temporary duty in Japan; why couldn't he just say sorry about that like anyone else? "Gomen don't get it, Lou." She hung up on him and turned her chair so she could stare out her office window, trying to hold back tears. "Goddamn it—"

Her door opened; there had been no knock. "God gave you knuckles," she snarled, turning, the anger she hadn't been able to lash at Lou begging to be unleashed on whoever had been brazen enough to enter uninvited.

"Your mail, Major." The rage and the hurt smoldering in Elen's eyes was as physical as an assault.

"What—?" She looked at what Elen had slapped to her desk and her stomach lurched. *They can't be here yet—oh god! they can't—* "Elen, I—" But she was talking to her back, and she didn't dare call after her; she was still sitting stunned five minutes later when came a roar of rage—"Son of a whore!"—and a dangerous crash. She heard Buckman's chair hit the back wall of his office as he launched; in a moment his door slammed and he asked in shaken amazement, "What in Christ is wrong with you, Mac? You could have killed someone!"

She gathered her control and went to the operations office to find the storm door flapping a tattered screen, the walkway beyond it sprayed with the shattered remains of Elen's coffee cup; Jerry Guzman's chest was soaked. "Was this an assault?" she asked neutrally.

"No, no." Hastily, he defended his section sergeant. "She started swearing and I came out to see what was going on and that fucking cup came through the air. Jesus, she's crazy when she's pissed."

"I see this." She looked at Elen's desk. The housing was removed from her typewriter, the empty reel of a fresh ribbon in place; the full spool was stretched across the office. That had been the first fling, she assumed, with no satisfactory crash; the cup had followed. She knew Elen's mother had taken a ceramics class just to make that mug with the loons on it. She put her hands in her pockets and sighed. "I'll write up an Article Fifteen," she murmured.

"Aw, Major, don't bust her. I'll never get any work out of her if you do."

She shrugged. "She's your clerk," she said, and left him gaping after her. When Dillinger said Article 15 people handed over their brass; she never backed down once the words were spoken. She stopped at the corner. "Have her clean up the mess and fix the door. And Jerry—" Faintly, she smiled. "Explain to her the difference between self-expression and totally unacceptable behavior."

"Jesus, that woman's weird," Jerry murmured, and got the broom and swept up the sidewalk himself. He knew Elen had loved that mug.

❏　　❏　　❏

"I cannot fucking believe you did that to me."

Kare opened her eyes. She hadn't heard a car in the driveway, or a door in the house, but here was Elen standing over her like a predator, her voice colder than dead and a copy of those goddamned orders crunched in her fist; it was past nine. She'd been lying on the sofa trying to put the fractured pieces of the day into place in her own heart; Elen hadn't shown at the gym, and when she wasn't home by eight Kare assumed she wouldn't be home at all. "Elen, I'm sorry," she said softly. "I never dreamed they'd come through this week."

"You never dreamed. That was kind of like finding my mother's obituary in the paper, Kare, to get your orders through distribution."

Kare sat up; she ran her hands through her hair and over her face and left them there. "I'm sorry," she whispered. "I don't know what else to say." She could feel the bristling aura of Elen's rage. A ruined screen and a shattered mug had only taken a temporary edge from it; that small violence had only kept her from disintegrating for a moment. Sickly, she wondered how much it would take to bring the pressure down this time. She waited.

"There's two things wrong with this picture," she heard at last; Elen's voice was like the dry, warning shimmer of a rattlesnake. "One is, you look like you expect me to hit you."

She couldn't deny it, in the silence after the words.

"The other one is, you look like you'd let me. And that hurts worse than you thinking I would in the first place."

She looked up. "Jesus, Elen! Your temper—"

"My temper?" Kare couldn't control the flinch when Elen's hand came toward her face; that touch was terribly gentle as fingertips traced across her cheek. "My temper might try to strain my coffee cup through a screen door, but it'll never lay a hand on you, and god damn you for thinking it would."

"Elen, if you're here to say goodbye, say it! I can't stand this. We both hurt enough. Please don't let us add to it."

"Why didn't you tell me?" Her voice was as gentle as her touch had been, a perverse and oddly insinuating caress of words. "How long have you known?"

"Since Thursday." It occurred to her that she was nearly terrified.

"Since Thursday. Kare, I'm not going to hit you." But Kare could take no reassurance in the words; that voice was too strange, too low, too calm. "Do you want me to leave?"

"No!" She broke; it was too much, too hard; Elen was too cold. "I want you not to be angry at me, Elen, I was trying to at least get an extension, that's why I didn't say anything, honey, I'd never have done that to you, not on purpose, please oh god Elen please believe me—"

She had never been made love to so gently, or so well; she allowed it even waiting for the fury, waiting for it to turn into a rape; she had never before had an orgasm that was part terror and part grief, leaving her sobbing into her lover's shoulder for knowing: now she would leave. But no hurtfulness came, and while she wept Elen held her, a deep embrace that felt precariously unsettled, and she awoke at first light with a hazy stress-hangover to find herself still held, Elen's fingers tracing through her hair in a slow, metronomic caress. She stirred, feeling that weird, dangerous gentleness tamed.

Lips touched her ear. "I'm sorry, Kare," Elen said softly. "Please know I'd never hurt you."

A sorrowed sigh shivered from her. "I wish I could still say that."

"You can. This was past your control, and my misunderstanding isn't your responsibility. Are we all right?"

"Oh, god, Elen—" Relief whispered through her. "We're all right. And I know you wouldn't. I know, Elen."

❏   ❏   ❏

"Package for you, Mac," said the mail clerk two weeks later, seeing her in the mess hall at lunch; Elen picked it up on her way back to work and sat at her desk to open the small, square box.

"I got a lovely note from your Major Dillinger with an apology that can best be described as abject for having knocked your mug off your desk," said her mother's smooth, round script. "She asked if I'd please make you another, since you were so fond of the first one. So here you are, dear. I can see why you speak of her so highly. She is both gracious and generous."

When Elen went smiling into Kare's office to confront her with the lie, an identical mug, filled with steaming coffee, sat on the blotter of Kare's desk.

❏   ❏   ❏

Elen didn't move in, precisely, but they blessed Kare's two-car garage for its ability to hide the fact that most nights Elen's car spent the night in Harker Heights instead of on post. Sometimes they spent the weekend at the house; sometimes they went to Austin or Dallas, Elen zooming Kare's smoke-windowed Porsche up or down I-35, Kare's hand resting on her thigh, her nails tracking softly against the inside seam of her jeans; it was as close as Elen would let her get. Kare had pretty much resigned herself to that.

They rarely spoke of Nikki Cole.

Weekdays, Elen found herself glancing too often at the loss roster hanging in her office. It was painful to move Kare from the ninety-day column to the sixty-day; on the Friday she hit the thirty-day list, Elen waited until the office had cleared except for the colonel and did it in tight-jawed privacy, unaware of Buckman leaning in his office door watching her, an unhappy frown in his eyes. He was having as much trouble writing Kare's final evaluation as Elen was having printing her name at the top of the thirty-day loss list. She was a splendid officer, and had made him an outstanding XO. If ever anyone deserved to trade gold oak leaves for the silver of light colonel, it was Kare, but—

But. Silently, he went back to his desk. "Maj. Dillinger is an exceptional officer with extraordinary knowledge of both transportation and supply," he wrote, and sighed, remembering how she had looked that morning out at West Fort Hood; he'd never been so sure any woman of his acquaintance had spent a night being thoroughly and exquisitely made love to, and the only other person who had looked smug that day was Elen McNally. Elen had deep-ended the day Kare's orders came through; "I'm homesick," she'd gritted when he asked why she'd come unglued. Now major and sergeant snarled at each other all week, frequently over whose loon mug was whose, when once they had seemed good friends— and now Elen looked like a twenty-mile forced march would be a preferable alternative to updating the loss roster. He looked up when Elen poked her head in his door. "Night, sir. Have a good weekend."

It blurted out of him. "Elen, are you and Kare sleeping together?"

She gaped at him in utter amazement—that much he would have expected—before she barked a disbelieving laugh. "Christ, sir! You need to take some of that leave time you've got stacked up."

"I asked a question." He watched her carefully. She looked incredulous, amused, a little insulted. To his knowledge (*I'm homesick and I'm on the rag and I hate the fucking*

Army! I hate it, Jesus, I hate the fucking Army—) she had never lied to him.

"Sir, with all due respect, it hardly deserves an answer."

"All the same, I'd like to hear one."

"No," she said gently. "No, Colonel. Major Dillinger and I aren't sleeping together. But that's one hell of a punchline; tell me the rest of the joke when you think it up, will you?" She eyed him with lingering, skeptical amusement. "Am I dismissed, sir?"

He eyed her, too, searching; steadily, she met his gaze. "Dismissed."

"Hoo," she said softly, shaking her head as she left his office. "Me and Dillinger? Boy howdy, Buckaroo. Time for you to go fishing, bro."

Buckman stared after her for a long moment before he picked up his pen.

"Her rapport with superiors is outstanding; upward loyalty from subordinates is unprecedented. Her intuition and foresight are remarkable. Exemplary dedication to duty, scrupulous attention to detail, and unparalleled leadership ability have contributed immeasurably to the successful completion of the missions of the battalion, brigade, and division. Without reservation, I recommend this officer for immediate promotion to lieutenant colonel and a battalion command."

Monday morning, he gave the draft to Elen to type. She returned it letter-perfect, word-for-word to the draft. "Glad she glows in the dark for someone," she said dryly. He pointed at his office door. She headed for the latrine to sag to the hopper, her head in her hands as she tried not to puke.

She hated having lied to him. Even reading his evaluation, she wasn't sure she had fooled him. She only knew Kare was safe.

❏   ❏   ❏

The last night Kare was rostered to be Deuce duty officer, Elen accepted ten bucks to relieve the duty driver and they cruised in the jeep, grateful for the time together. The moon was nearly full; once when she looked over, she saw the glitter of silent tears on Kare's face. She killed the engine and lights behind a fuel pumping station they had legitimate reason to visit. "Tell me," she said softly. "Don't do it alone when I'm here with you."

Kare's voice was soft, unsteady. "Elen, do you love me?"

"Oh, god—yes, Kare. I do."

"Then why won't you let me touch you?" It was an anguished cry. "All the time we've been together you've never let me make love to you! Elen, you're driving me crazy with this! You're a beautiful lover, and I love to have you make love to me, but god! my pleasure isn't enough. I feel selfish, Elen, I—"

"Kare, don't. You know I come—"

"You tell me you do. You say it makes you crazy to feel me wet, but you deny me that. You say you love the taste of me, and you deny me that—I can't believe you love me. Not when you have to call all the shots. Not when you can't let me be equal as your lover."

"You knew the first night—"

"You said you were all right and I believed you. You didn't say you'd never let me touch you."

"I can't! And I can't explain it—god, please try to understand."

"How much does it have to do with Nikki?"

"Nik—? Kare, no. Nothing."

"Can you tell me you don't still love her?"

"No, I can't. Whatever she never was to me, Kare, she was my friend, but she doesn't—she's never—come between us. God, where is this coming from?"

"We've got seventeen days. And I want you—" She glared at the sky, at the stars and the shadow of Blackwell Mountain. "Elen, I want to touch you. I need to know you love me, I need to know you trust me, I need to know—" She choked back the rest of it.

"Say it," Elen said softly.

She drew a shaky breath. "I need to know I'm not just in place of her."

"Oh, god—" Elen leaned into the steering wheel, giving it her hurt; she felt the shallow, sipping breaths of that pain, a sharpness like broken ribs. "Oh, no. Jesus, Kare, I love you. Why can't you believe me?"

"How can I? You don't trust me enough to let me—"

"Wait," she whispered. "Please. Let me—" She fumbled for a cigarette, but the smell of fuel underlined the night; she jammed the pack back into her pocket. "Let me sort this out," she begged. "Love me a few minutes more."

Last night. She had tried; god, she had tried to let Kare touch her, but gentle as her hand had been, when it slipped between her thighs she had frozen, choking on something that felt like panic and rage and some dark, murderous instinct; she had fled the bed, knowing she was hurting Kare, unable to stop herself. "I've got to pee," she'd managed, and did that and went to the dining room for a shooter of scotch, and went back to the bedroom to find Kare pretending to be asleep, unresponsive when she touched her, and neither of them had slept; they laid there wearily wakeful, aching to talk, to heal, neither of them knowing where to start.

"Kare," she said now, softly, "I don't know how much you knew about me before that day you hauled me out from under that truck—"

"I knew who you were." Her voice said she would try.

"I was fucking my way through the battalion," Elen whispered. "Thank god most of them are gone now. Hogle was last because he hurt me, but . . . Kare, they all did. They helped me hurt myself. They didn't care about me any more than I did. When Hogle—I told myself—I—I know I'm hurting you but I can't—I get so scared, Kare, I—he hurt me and I know you won't but god, I don't know how—I was trying to protect myself, saying I'd never let—no one. I said no one like it was a prayer and I hate it now, I hate this but I—and I'm scared, Kare, I'm so afraid to lose you, you—"

"Elen, no. Honey, I love you. You won't lose me."

"—mean everything to me and you're" —*leaving me.* "If you can't—if I can't—oh, fuck," she wept, and stopped trying to talk, to explain; she just tried not to cry.

"Elen—" Kare touched her shoulder, her hair, wishing they were in bed, wishing she could hold her. "Oh, Elen. I'm so sorry, honey."

"It's me. You didn't do anything."

"I pressured the hell out of you—" A choked laugh slipped from her. "Too late. Elen, all we need is time, and god, we don't have it. Let me get you a tour in Germany. Come with me. If I put in the paperwork tomorrow we won't be more than a month apart—"

"Kare, Jesus! I can't follow you to Germany without them knowing we're lovers! I'll ruin your career, you're looking at a star—"

"I'm looking at our lives! My god, you can't do it this way—honey, I'm not saying I'm the only one who can help, I'm only saying that if we had time we could get through this.

We're fighting because we don't want to be apart and there's no way out of it—unless you come with me. My orders are cut, Elen. I have to go. If you reenlisted—"

"Reenlist?" She looked at Kare in wonder. "No, Kare. I hate the Army."

"Honey, do you hate the Army, or what happened to you here? It isn't all Fort Hood, it isn't all the Deuce—all I got out of three years here is you and Elen, I don't want to lose you. You're the best thing that's ever happened to me. Please come with me."

"Oh, god—Kare, I can't," she whispered. "I get out in December. I'll go to Germany as a civilian, but god, don't ask me to reenlist. Please."

"Elen, that's nine months! I don't want to be without you that long."

"Do you think I do? Kare, if I re-up I'll end up hating you. I'd rather lose you clean than lose you that way."

That hurt; Kare tried to hide it and knew she hadn't when Elen reached for her.

"I'm sorry," she said softly. "Kare, I'm not like you. What rolls off your back beats me half to death. I'm not wired right for the military. I can hold my breath for nine months, but not—"

Kare kissed her; it wasn't wanting to as much as it was wanting not to hear her say no. Elen's lips parted under hers, her tongue almost hesitant in seeking the warmth inside her mouth, and a poignancy of loving her, of missing her before she was gone, diffused in her. "Make love to me," she whispered against that gentle mouth. "Right here, Elen. Right now."

And in the back seat of the jeep, with slow, consummate ability, Elen did, as if she wanted to take as much as she could of the little time they had left. Kare had never loved so deeply, or known she was so loved, and when finally they were regaining their breaths with their lips barely touching and Elen's hand still cupping her in gentle possession, she pushed the hair away from Elen's forehead, her thumb tracing the thin scar there. "Oh, my love," she whispered, touching her lips to that pale mark. "At least I know you'll never forget me."

CHAPTER NINE

"Yo, Miss Lady. What it is?"

Elen glanced up from the pool table to see Jim Baines, the reenlistment NCO; she drew back her cue and stroked. The six-ball banked twice into a side pocket. "Cost you ten bucks to find out." The dayroom had been empty but for her on a hot September Saturday afternoon. After a month of sixteen-hour days preparing for the annual general inspection and then a grueling week of the inspection itself, the troops of the Deuce had exploded from the barracks like birdshot from a double-barreled twelve-gauge; Monday's morning report would be peppered with AWOLs. She tapped a corner with her stick to show where she'd sink the seven; the ball clattered into the already-occupied pocket.

"Ain't but a fool put money against you, girl," he grinned, "an' I know you don't never play for fun."

The nine-ball dropped. "No guts, no glory, no purple hearts. What else d'you know?"

"I know I need one more lifer-type to re-up to make my quota this quarter. Cap'n says he sure wish it'd be you."

"Tell the captain if wishes and buts were apples and nuts we'd all have a merry Christmas." She sank the stripes in order, and then the eight, and began picking balls from the pockets, rolling them all to one end. "Grab a stick; I'll give you a free lesson. Why the hell would I reenlist, Jimbo?"

He chose and chalked. "Beautiful downtown Europe and a serious bonus?"

She snorted a laugh. "I've got sixty-nine days and a wake-up. You ain't got nothin' serious enough to change that, bro." She scooped the balls into the rack and centered the black one.

"The bro's talkin' ten grand, little mama," he said quietly. "And I can guarantee you Heidelberg."

She looked up from the rack, her fingers frozen on the balls.

Gently, indulgently, he smiled. "Just you an' her an' a Porsche an' the autobahn, baby. Just like old times."

She lifted the rack and hung it; she broke down her cue and tucked it into its case and closed the latches. At the door of the dayroom she turned. "I'll tell the captain you tried, Jim," she said gently. "And I'll tell him the same thing I'm telling you, man: leave it alone. I've got sixty-nine days and a wake-up before happiness is Fort Hood Texas in my rear-view mirror."

"You might's well go with money in yo' pocket, girl— 'cause I'm knowin' where you're goin' when you're gone. Ten grand, baby; in yo' hand."

Faintly, she smiled. "Brother Baines, what you don't know about me would fill a hell of a lot fatter book than what you think you know."

She scuffed down the hall to Room 104 and locked herself in. The four Grolsches in her little refrigerator had been planned for later tonight; she snapped a bottle from the rack and thumbed the wire bail, flipping open the ceramic stopper. "One," she said, and tipped the bottle back.

One for Nikki Cole, two years gone today.

One for Rae Vitale, dead a year and a month.

One for Kare Dillinger, in Heidelberg six months.

And one for Elen McNally, because three of those stout sixteen-ouncers weren't quite enough to put her out.

For the first two months Kare's letters had come almost daily. Then time between them started to stretch, and Elen's heart stretched with it, thinner and thinner until it seemed it had to break—and then a letter would come to save her for another week . . . or ten days. Or two weeks. Or month.

Colonel Buckman was gone. When he'd left the Deuce, he had presented Elen with a good imitation of an Oscar statuette: Best Actress *Elen McNally* in *Punchline*, and Elen knew she admitted the lie when she didn't refuse the award for it. It had been funny then; then, Kare had still been writing every other day.

She looked at the golden figurine on top of her locker. "Yeah, Bucky," she whispered. "Yeah, that was one hell of a punchline. How come you never told me I was the fucking joke?"

❏   ❏   ❏

Kare and Nikki and Rae were gone; Colonel Buckman and Captain Guzman and Lieutenant Gouda were gone. Jeannie, Trapp, Iver, PJ—all of them were gone. Only she and Luke Czosnik were left of the old Deuce crew; if she went to the motor pool, from tool shack to birdbath she didn't know anyone. No one else remembered the day BB Cole put the squeeze to ol' Hogle; if she said Chuckie Cheeseballs she got only blank looks. Was the horror of seeing Rae Vitale's raped and murdered body being bagged and loaded into the belly of a chopper out in West Fort Hood still fresh in only two memories? Did no one else remember General Patton, or the day President Carter had come to call? "Damn, Luke," she said when she saw Czosnik next. "We need to have us a brew for the old times. We're king and queen here, and I'm a two-digit midget."

They absconded with a jeep and a six-pack and headed for the range, for those tank trails where so many beers had been drunk, so many joints smoked, so many lives shared. "I remember the day you came here, Mac." Luke Czosnik's tattooed snake slithered around his wrist as he twisted the cap from a beer for her. "What happened to the rest of them? I remember the day Nikki Cole put the ol' squeeze to that Hogle. Didn't he cry, yah? You ever hear from her, Mac? You were good friends, you and her."

"No, Top," she said softly. "No, I never do."

❑   ❑   ❑

I did it wrong. She stood on a bridge overlooking the Aroostook River on 8 December 1978, staring down the frozen stretch of it.

She had written to Kare to say she was a thirty-day loss with money to get to Germany, but she had felt perfunctory in the writing; she knew now she must have sounded that way. After eight months she'd guessed she understood how good for a while didn't mean good forever, especially with a woman chasing a star. "I'll always love you," she closed the letter, and meant it, but she knew she meant goodbye if that was what Kare wanted to hear, and she waited a long time for a few words.

You can't know how much I want to see you, Elen, but it's just not good right now. The fans and the shit are too close together. But keep in touch—that's an order. They won't be too close forever, and I always want to know where you are. I love you, too, Squirt. Believe it.

So she hugged Luke Czosnik goodbye; five hours later she left Texas behind her. Three days later she rang Henry Cole's doorbell. "Please tell me where Nikki is. Please. This is my life, here."

"Your needs concern me not at all, Ms. McNally," he said coldly. "You've got thirty seconds to get out of my driveway before I call the police."

It took him more like thirty minutes to get rid of her, and for many of those minutes they were nose to nose, but at midnight, tight-jawed, dry-eyed, numb with fatigue, she crossed the Piscataqua River into Maine. She drove on autopilot, no feelings or memories intruding for the last seven of twenty hours on the road. She staggered into her parents' house and collapsed, and slept twenty hours and woke up wondering what in god's name she was going to do with the rest of her life.

Somehow she'd never thought any farther: as her hopes of Germany faded, she had known she'd confront Henry, find Nikki, and they'd go for that beer. And then life would go on—with Nikki.

But there was no Nikki. There had only been six months of Nikki, six months and a letter that may have been truth when it was written but sounded like a lie now, a maybe she had allowed to cost her Kare: without it, she'd not have asked if Kare wanted her to go to Germany. She simply would have gone.

"Oh, god," she whispered, sitting on the edge of her bed at home, her face in her hands and Kare's memory so potent in her heart it made Nikki feel like a shadow. "God, what did I do? What have I given up? Kare—"

She opened the tiny Lane cedar chest she'd gotten when she graduated from high school; Nikki's letter was there, its edges frayed, its folds fragile. She opened it and let her eyes touch the old familiar words. *Elen, my love. I wish I could have faced you but it would have killed me to say goodbye to you.*

"It never occurred to you that it might almost kill me that you didn't?" But she was gentle with that faded piece of paper when she folded it again; she tried to resist the other letter there, and couldn't.

You can't know how much I want to see you.

She laughed, a small, hurt laugh. "I know how much," she whispered. "Not enough, Goddess; that's how much."

She closed the little chest, and dressed and went to tug her coat from the hall closet. "I'm going up to the university," she told her mother. "See what the spring semester looks like."

But first, she went to the river. The Army-issue overcoat kept the wind from her body, but the tears froze on her face.

No goodbyes. Not ever; not for us. I love you, too—

Bitterly, she smiled. "Yeah," she murmured. "Yeah, I love you, too."

CHAPTER TEN

"You're asking me to allow you to carry twenty-one hours and I don't know you from Mother Goose." Elen didn't need Nikki to tell her that the professor she had been assigned as an advisor was a dyke. Like Nikki, she was five-foot- three and had brown hair, and that was the end of the resemblance. The brown hair was an inch long, and the five-three packed a hundred and sixty solid pounds; there were lines of dirt under ragged fingernails, and coffee stains on her shirt. In the Army she would have been a master sergeant, that tough and crusty breed, capable and relentless; master sergeants had been cigar smokers in Elen's observation, and this professor had a brown cigarette corked into a corner of her mouth, squinting against the blue plume it was trying to send under thumb-smudged glasses that looked as if she sat on them regularly. Around her hips was a military pistol belt studded with a sheath knife, a cased pair of mini-binoculars, and canvas ammo pouches filled with god-knew-what; there was a conjure bag at her neck, bulging with amulets and secrets. Her desk was a fantastic jumble of books and papers, over-whelmed ashtrays, many pipes, a half-eaten sandwich, an ax, odd small statuary; the rest of her office threatened to explode under its load of books and papers. "Not just twenty-one hours, Ms. McNally, but fifteen of them English and Ed courses. Do you have any concept of how much reading we're talking about?"

The professor hadn't offered her a seat. Elen stood relaxed, her fingers tucked into the pockets of her jeans; it was the old talking-to-Kare-if-others-could-see stance, not too familiar, to befit her rank, but not too stiff, to show the ease of respect. "I read very well, Dr. Pinero and I have excellent retention." There was no helping the tiny grin that seemed stuck to her face; this dyke was a treasure. Six of the twenty-one hours Elen had requested would be from her—if the professor approved.

"How old are you, Elen McNally?"

"I'm twenty-two, ma'am."

"Ma'am? You call me ma'am? What are you, in the damn Army?"

"Until two weeks ago. I served three years. I was a good soldier and I mean to be a good student, but I'd like to make this university thing a three-year hitch—with your indulgence, ma'am."

"I'll indulge your butt with my foot if you call me ma'am again." She scrawled a signature on Elen's course request. "I hope you're as good as you think you are, McNally. That cocky grin looks good on you, but at twenty-one hours a semester I've got doubts about how long you'll wear it. Dismissed."

It was too abruptly military; Elen snapped to attention and saluted before she could catch it. Pinero's laughter followed her down the hall. Elen smiled tightly. *Yuk it up. When you can pull down a seventy-two hour shift without sleep, eating cold C rations and chasing rattlesnakes, range bulls, and the First Cavalry Division all over West Fort in 110-degree weather, grab three hours of sketchy Zs on top of a footlocker before you find a dead friend and nail down seventy-two even longer hours, let me know, Pinero. When you can drive the woman you love to the airport and salute her instead of kiss her when she walks out of your life, let me know. I've got my GI Bill and money in the bank, and it'll take more than a stack of textbooks to crack the grin, baby.*

Nina Pinero leaned back in her chair, a smile crinkling her black Sicilian eyes. That tall, cool drink of water would rise like cream; Nina had known that in the first fifteen seconds. Elen McNally had just the right shade of Self in her smile, just the right way of wearing that military topcoat over jeans and a sweater and boots still shiny from the last inspection—and just enough fresh, simmering pain in her heavy-lidded hazel eyes: not enough to bow her, but enough to allow her the vision. "I'll make you cry, McNally, and I'll make you thank me for it. Sharpen your pencil, girl."

❏   ❏   ❏

Dr. Pinero watched those boots all semester, expecting the shine to dull under a lack of time to maintain it; it didn't. Monday mornings at eight the heels and toes of the jump boots glowed like onyx; Thursday evenings at six-thirty they winked and gleamed like an amused Sicilian eye. "Write for two hours about anything you want," she said one night ten weeks into her freshman composition course, after a lecture that had wandered with apparent aimlessness around simile and metaphor, euphemism and symbolism. "Except you, McNally. You write about those boots of yours."

Elen regarded her with that almost amused, almost maddening grin, and looked at her feet for all of thirty seconds before she uncapped a broad-nibbed Waterman pen and began to write. Pinero watched her: there was no pen-chewing, no head-scratching; once in a while she looked up and out, considering some distant thing beyond the walls, a finger caressing a thin scar on her forehead. Fifteen seconds, perhaps, or thirty, passed before the pupils of those smoky hazel eyes dilated in understanding or realization and her pen began to move, laying down great chunks of words before that gathering pause would come again. She ran out of ink once, and reloaded her pen with an efficiency that suggested jamming a fresh magazine into a hot M-16; it didn't cost her ten seconds.

"Time," Pinero said at nine-thirty. Elen wrote a dozen more words and a period and creased her paper lengthwise and gave it to the professor's hand like an operating room nurse handing the surgeon a scalpel.

"Within the duality of me rides the soles of a being," Nina read that night, and groaned, but the five pages of neat, aggressive all-caps printing told a tightly-constructed tale of six days of ethereal hell spent in the warped frame of three hours of mid-point sleep. The boots felt the creeping exhaustion of their wearer; they swelled in cold nights and shrank in hot days, jittered in nervousness, kicked in frustration, thirsted in the dust and choked in the wind-driven rain.

"O, forgive these clumsy feet that wear us, forgive the blindness of our eyes that we did not see this hand we've walked on—O gods and goddess this is our friend! our friend and she is O she is dead, this hand we've trampled that so many times caressed us, O Rae, how brief the glow you gave us! How can you lie in dirt we claim as our domain? O knees, join us; feel with us the pain of stones that scar us, know the unforgiving Mother that holds her now above Her, so soon to cradle this shining friend in Her cool and crumbling arms—"

❑   ❑   ❑

European Literature. "Write," Dr. Pinero said. "Two hours."

"Some mental masturbation re: *Madame Bovary*.
"Emma, Emma. Would that you had ever learned that
the hole in your soul had so little to do with the one between
your legs! If only you had realized that a firm phallus was not
the answer to your firmness of mind, that those 'loves' of
yours were but diversions designed to take from you the truth
of yourSelf. You would have been better off going to Paris,
learning interior design, having a satisfaction, a celebration
of self, a life's-work; had you only known that you could *be*,
without a man to tell you what and how and who to be. What
a madam you'd have made! You could have rivaled Kate in
East of Eden, no one's favorite character but mine, I think;
Adam did with Kathy what Charles has done with you,
keeping you on a filthy pedestal for him and his cronies to
admire without regard for your wishes or for your very being;
Kathy/Kate escaped as best she could and found success
where her youthful torment led her. Steinbeck kept her hard
and bitter and I think he was wrong (dare I criticize the
master? Betcher ass); he worked from the perspective of the
phallocracy, discarding his own theme of Choice; did he
mean Choice only to apply happily to the males in his
masterpiece? She'd have made a mighty merry dyke, stroking
the men away from their money and laughing all the way to
the bank!

"But I digress. I've been many of the places you have,
Emma. I've been in the place where another's drawn breath
was an infringement upon my right to the air; I've been where
another's touch was a rape of my body, and a look was a rape
of my soul; I've been where the inside of the place called
Home was filled with a choking liquid atmosphere that threatened to drown me in its oppression, where a word was
grounds for abandonment if not murder—even the most
well-intentioned and truly loving word. I've been where the

love of another made me cry to rip off my clothes and swim
stark into the sea, out and out and out until further out is the
only option left; I've stood at the edge of that sea and watched
my other self do that, my real self wearing a tight thin smile
that made my lover question my thoughts, the question making me turn my eyes away for knowing one loved and one
couldn't. And I saw that lover in the same space; it does work
both ways, Emma, after you kill the love, or after it dies on
its own. And I've seen my realization that I can be content in
mySelf. That's what you needed, Emma: yourSelf. I know it
wasn't fashionable in your time, in your place, for women to
have selves, but you did have one, had you only looked for
it, discovered or uncovered it, had you only been able to
slough off the layers of your father and your husband and his
hateful spiteful mother, and even Leon, with which you were
cloaked, the layers of custom and tradition and normalcy.
Goddess, save me from normalcy! Can you see it was only
more acceptable for you to go to the arms of other men than
it would have been for you to go alone? Can you see you were
playing their game when your soul was screaming for your
own game, your own rules? Can you see I am talking not only
to a fictional person, but to a dead fictional person?"

❏   ❏   ❏

More European lit: *Faust*. "Write," the professor said.
"Two hours."
"Sure," grumbled the kid beside Elen at the table. "We
work, she sits somewhere and smokes. Tough fuckin' gig
she's got, that old dyke."
"You write for two hours, pinhead; so do I, so do sixteen
other people in this course and she's got five. How long does
it take her to read it all? Shut up and lick your pencil. Your
daddy makes your car payments, doesn't he?"

"Fuck you, bitch!"

"You won't be man enough to fuck me in this reign of Christ, Jeff." It wasn't her words that shriveled him; it was the utter, contemptuous boredom in her gold-flecked hazel eyes.

"Musings on *Faust*:

"Shades of Mark Twain. Seems a lot of thinking people ponder the way gods treat mortals. Does the fact that we *are* mortal have bearing on the literary questions being so frequently posed by the personage of the fallen angel? How would Gretchen's downfall in *Faust* fit with Twain's concept of fate as described by Satan in *The Mysterious Stranger*? Had Faust not interfered with her life when he did, would she have lived a long and miserable time, so better to get the misery over with quickly? Could the same then be said of my sister Erin, who simply didn't wake up one morning of her fifteenth year? It's small consolation to the living to ponder the nature of destiny even as we attempt to comprehend the reality of death.

"Why does God—in literature, which raises the whole 'nother question of divine inspiration, in the Book of Job if not the Book of Faust—single out individual mortals for testing? Is this just part of his great experiment as described in *Letters From the Earth*, or are we all pissing in our shoes? Is this a crapshoot to God, are he and Satan hanging around the pool hall selling drugs to school children, or are we mortals naught but pawns in his attempt to demonstrate to Satan that in the end good will triumph over evil, in hopes that he may convince Satan and Mephistopheles (should we take those two literally as two, or are they a symbolic unified entity?) to see the error of his/their ways and return to God's fold, as the prodigal son? "Hey Rafe, Gabe, let's roast a goat; ol' Scratch is home to stay."

"And why are there so many nicknames for the devil? *Absit nomen, absit omen*—avoid the name and avoid the curse, the saying goes, but Beelzebub, Cloot, Lucifer, ol' Gooseberry, ol' Scratch, ol' Nick, Himself; do people think he doesn't learn his newly-awarded aliases as fast as we think them up?

"Is it okay just to ask questions, or must I attempt to formulate answers? Is it as important to have all of the answers as some of the questions?

"Why does Faust put up with Wagner, the 'crawling pedant'? Wagner is roots, Faust is wings; does Faust keep him in sight the way people keep an urn full of ashes on the mantelpiece, as a reminder of mortality? Wagner is an example of intellectual limitation the way an ash-filled urn is of physical likewise. Is Wagner a catalyst, the concept of his Self so horrifying to Faust that he would entertain in the first place the notion of wagering with Mephistopheles?

"And I don't like the idea of God and Mephisto betting with a man's soul. At least in a horse race you don't kill the losing nag, bet on him or even with him though you may. Faust's soul is offered into hell for one mistake, sealed in blood and waited for with bated breath: 'Linger a while; thou art so fair!' What exquisite words, to condemn a soul to dark eternity!

("If God were suddenly condemned to live the life which He has inflicted upon men, He would kill Himself." —Alexandre Dumas fils)

"When I read Solon's words to Croesus, wherein he theorized no man could be called happy until he had seen the end of his days, I thought, this Solon is a wise dude. The way gods jumped around in people's knickers in his time, it was well to wait and see what divine intervention had in store before you yodeled about how lucky and happy you were. Divine intervention in Greek-godly method is hardly fair, but this divine gambling is considerably less fair.

"Alas. At the ripe old age of five, having lost a dear grandparent and thus faced with the brutal abstraction of mortality, I started to comprehend that fairness was a concept rife with suspect; when I was thirteen my older sister died, and I knew fairness was a good idea but it'd never play in Peoria; now I find the whole thing bitterly amusing. Were life fair and people did what they said they'd do, I'd be in Germany; accumulation would be the way the game was played were any god a just one, and to hell with 'one strike and you're out and here's to your ol' lady, too.'

"Alas, indeed. By the time you get done with me, Dr. P., I'll be returned to the philosophical level I entertained at sixteen: believing in a higher power only because someone had to light the fuse to the dynamite (and that a point to be debated with Nikki as we worked our way through a pint of vodka on a Texas Saturday night, me taking the view that friction causes sparks and sparks are energy and energy is synonymous with life, Nikki maintaining that before there is friction there has to be something to rub together and where did *that* come from, you smart-assed Mainiac? *Ad infinitum, ad nauseam.*)

"Perhaps I'll simply remain amused."

"Aha," Nina Pinero murmured. "At last the curse has a name."

CHAPTER ELEVEN

The normal mortals of Aroostook, Maine's north-ernmost county, found July's heat stifling; Elen, three Texas summers still in her blood, sailed through ninety-degree days looking crisp and cool and irritating everyone around her. With only twelve summer hours at university she felt time-laden; she discovered a marvelous bartender at the Chinese restaurant in town and whiled away her evenings there, sparring with Larry when he had time, reading when he didn't, taking notes on paper placemats. The manager shook his head over her; she didn't look right at the table in the corner, spit-shined boots propped on a chair, nose in a book, blonde hair glinting in the dim lights, smoke curling in a blue halo around her head, but she always had a vodka (she had tried to drink scotch, but it made her think of Kare, and Kare hadn't answered her last two letters) on the table, and Larry confirmed her good-customer status for both food and drink.

Men would watch her, and approach her only to have their hearts jump-started and then stalled again by a look that was heavy-lidded and sensual and as mercilessly cold as an Aroostook February, and they would creep back to their drinks wondering how a smile and a shake of the head could make them feel as if their balls had been wrapped in barbed wire and packed in shards of ice.

And women watched her, and saw her send the men away with that sultry, dangerous smile, and some of the women approached her; sometimes she lifted her feet from the second chair at her table so the woman could sit, and they would talk, but when her drink was empty she would say nice talking with you, and gather her book and her notes and leave. Larry watched her, too, with a sad and tight-lipped smile.

It was the evening 16 July, while she was engrossed in *Mrs. Stevens Hears the Mermaids Singing*, that a familiar voice said quietly, "Tell me about Nikki," and she looked up in precipitous wariness to find Nina Pinero in hat and full-gear pistol belt; absurdly, she remembered it had been 16 July when the trucker from A Company had driven her to the edge of a motel room bed and sodomized her into a weird and unwanted sort of celibacy that had lasted—*happy anniversary, Elen*—three years tonight.

"Your timing's exquisite, Dr. Pinero." She lifted her feet from the second chair. "Three years ago tonight my life was entering the dimension that would allow her. Tell me the nature of three."

Dr. Pinero grinned. "Now, you know I could go on at great length about the nature of trinity: symbolism and mysticism and metaphysical context. You know if I could be enticed to do that, you wouldn't have to answer my question."

Elen smiled, too. "Indeed. Would it be easier, do you think, for me to entice you into the nature of trinity, or for you to entice me into the nature of Nikki? May I buy you a drink while we debate the nature of enticement?"

"Another diversionary tactic, which I will accept via half a carafe of white wine. Larry! the usual over here, twice. You're reading May Sarton."

"A trick I learned from Nikki: pick an author and read in chronological order. She left Sarton, Stein, and Twain, when she left me. I'm just recently able to indulge myself in Sarton. How did you know to ask about her?"

"Your handwriting tripped over the pain. What happened three years ago?"

"I was raped," she said quietly. "She helped me heal."

"But you've never healed from her."

Elen lifted her hands, a tiny shrug.

"Do you write, except when you're asked to?"

"For myself." *Letters to Kare, who probably doesn't even read them.*

"Do you have any idea how good you are? Are you going to piss yourself away diagramming sentences for eighth-graders?"

"I thought this was about Nikki."

"Is it easier to talk about a pain so great than it is to talk about yourself? Tell me about her, then."

Elen tasted the drink Larry had brought her. It was freshly pungent with alcohol. She selected a cigarette and tapped the filter against the table and finally lit it; she aimed a thin stream of smoke at the floor and looked up and said softly, "Forgive me, for I have sinned. Yes, confession would ease the soul; it would be an immense relief to confess to one I know would understand and be able to help me understand. But I might want to write it someday." That lazy smile was edged with something hollow, almost brittle. "May Sarton said in an essay on the design of a novel that the reason for writing a novel is that the writer is bothered by something she needs to understand, that the writing of the novel is the process of understanding. If I understand now, Dr. Pinero, I've lost my novel."

An implacable smile curved onto Dr. Pinero's lips. "Then we'll talk about Elen. What are you going to do with that ed degree?"

"I'd thought about teaching." Elen grinned, that tiny grin she wore in class that said come on, hit me with your best shot. "Specifically, diagramming sentences to eighth-graders. Or maybe diagramming Flaubert to precocious university freshmen who think they're smart enough to take upper-level courses —and who are smart enough to bullshit their advisor into letting them."

Larry threw them out at midnight; Elen left her car and walked with the older woman, now Nina, up the long hill to the street where the professor kept a house. The professor's questions were often twenty minutes long, woven with threads she never seemed to lose the ends of, and Elen answered as briefly as possible just to free the airtime. Listening to her was a short course in three or seven or ten fields at once: literature and history and philosophy, theology, metaphysics, cultural abstraction, mysticism, music.

"Consider the nature of aristocracy: the man on horseback versus the man on foot," Nina said, when Elen locked and left her car, and there followed a meticulous dissection of concept that scooped up self-image, classism, mob instinct, dallied with sexism when a carful of teenage boys razzed them on the way by, returned to mob instinct—"the tendency of the oppressed to align themselves with their oppressors; you saw that in the Army"—and the psychology of role reversal, until Elen despaired of putting them all together and prayed there wasn't going to be a pop quiz. And with a seamless finish Dr. Pinero wove those dangling threads into a rich tapestry and said, "You should think about things like that sometimes. This is my house. Your body is lovely but I have no interest in it; it's your intellect I want to seduce. Will you come in? I'll make espresso."

It was late; she was lightly oiled on vodka chased with Frangelico. There would be looks from her mother in the

morning. The fingers of the night breeze were cool against
her skin; three years ago tonight she had been sitting in her
car on the Blackwell Mountain Road sucking rum from the
neck of a bottle, crying, smoking, finally puking, finally going
back to Room 104 to find Nikki Cole, who would lead her to
Kare. "Tell me about trinity," she said quietly, "and I'll tell
you about the day Nikki put the squeeze to ol' Hogle."

❏   ❏   ❏

*Dear Kare: I hate this, I hate missing you, I hate it that
I've lost you, I hate being without you, why did you*
"Shit," she muttered, and crumpled the page.

Dearest Kare: Linger a while, thou art . . .
". . . so fair? She'll think you're fucking nuts" —she
shot the balled sheet of paper at the wastebasket by her desk—
"and be right."

*OK, Goddess, separate your shit and your fans. I'm
coming to Germany. I can't stand this. I have to see you. If it
hurts your career, too ba*

*Dear Kare: You never believed I loved you, did you. I
wonder how I ever believed you loved me. I hope you're happy
with your star when you get it; don't let the sharp points cause
you as much pain as you've caus*

*Dear Kare: Dear, my ass. Fuck you and the horse you
rode*

*Goddess, I'm lying here naked wishing I had my tongue
in your*
"No. No, Elen. No, no, no. Jesus."

Dear Kare: I talked to a friend tonight, told her all about Nikki and nada about you. I couldn't confess; I couldn't admit I'm doing it again, driving myself crazy loving someone who doesn't love me, but I know you did once and this is killing me. What did I do? What's wrong with me that people I love, who supposedly love me, always leave me hang

Dear Mr. Pepys: And so to bed. Kare Dillinger, you can go to hell.

CHAPTER TWELVE

"May I infringe upon what's feeling very much like a friendship to ask you a question of excruciating rudeness, Ms. Nina?" she asked one night in November as they walked up the hill from the hotel bar towards Nina's house; her voice was smooth under the lubrication of several rounds of top-shelf vodka and their usual last call of Frangelico. "Knowing, of course, that a question of any description is something you can't seem to resist answering."

"You haven't noticed my propensity for answering questions with questions when I question whether the question is one I'd choose to answer?"

"Indeed, Gertrude—and I've noticed the question you ask in response to a question you don't want to answer is sometimes more revealing than the answer would have been. Why is it only my mind you've tried to seduce?"

"An excruciatingly rude question indeed, displaying the almost unforgivable arrogance of raw youth. Sometimes I forget you're only twenty-two, McNally."

"I was twenty-three two weeks ago. Just for the record."

"Sometimes I forget you're only twenty-three, McNally, and prone to that insufferable arrogance that's an inevitable result of firm thighs and flat bellies and minds that remember why you've gone to the store. Because we're too much alike."

Elen stopped in mid-stride. "Excuse me?"

Indulgently, Nina laughed. "That's the first time I've ever surprised you, McNally! Listen: you choose to be celibate, as do I, but you're sexual; you're one of the most sexual women I've ever met. You seethe with it. You drive men crazy, and I know women at the university who'd sacrifice major body parts if only you'd approach them. I'm not one of them, although I understand the look in their eyes when they look at you; twenty years ago I might have plied my position to gain unconscionable advantage over you. Why, it's your arrogance that's so appealing. You've openly embraced the difference of which your Nikki spoke when she spoke to you of loving women; you grasp that difference, intimately and innately, on its intellectual levels—but you politicize and romanticize and call it a lifestyle as if it were a choice. You're one of the most respected radical lesbian feminists on campus, and yet you have so little experience in the day-to-day emotional and physical intimacies that comprise a real-world lesbian relationship—why, you're virtually a virgin. I can't tell you how that amuses me—and how at the same time it so deeply disturbs me."

They walked; uneasily, Elen wondered why she had never told Nina about Kare. "If I'd approach them?" she finally asked. "Why don't they approach me?"

"McNally! You are so assertively butch no self-respecting femme would even consider approaching you for fear of wounding your hubris and then being in the way of the result. The aura of your personal intensity, into which you let so few intrude, is almost as wide as your shadow is long in this streetlamp. They're afraid of being burned by the heat."

"But—Nina, I don't think of myself as butch. I'm not into role-playing."

"Look at yourself in a mirror, McNally! No good; you'll see through your own eyes. I'm your mirror. Do you see tall and slim and blonde? Adjust this for gender: 'yond Cassius has a lean and hungry look; he thinks too much: such men are dangerous.' You have the look of a predator about you, an essence of danger —not violence, but danger, chance, risk— and at the same time, you have the bearing of gentleness. You have a way of holding your head that dares the world to hit you with its best shot—and warns that your best shot will be duly returned, and will be a shot to be reckoned with. At the same time there's an amusement that says you know the game is silly, all this shooting and hitting; we've all been hurt before and none of us enjoyed it then, you suggest, so let's have a cup of tea and talk like civilized folk. Your style of dress, with those long flowing coats and trim woolen pants and sensuous sweaters and snap-brim Stetson fedoras—why, it's unique and in extraordinarily good taste, but no one else could get away with those ridiculous boots—except me."

"Except you, indeed," Elen muttered. "On three or four levels, you're practically describing yourself, Nina."

"I said we were too much alike, didn't I? Here's the difference: you're a beautiful woman—but if you could grow a mustache you'd be a handsome man. You revel so deeply in your androgyny that others admire you for it—and I'm not contradicting my earlier self who said men lust after you. They do; they want to tame you. Those women want to tame you. As do I—but it's that unruly mind of yours I'm after. You see, Elen, only you and I know how very, very deeply you are owned. You're owned the way a fine dog is owned: you could buy a dog and own it and not have much of a dog, or you could come upon a dog who would volunteer its Self to you, its entirety of loyalty and love and devotion, as you've volunteered yourself to her . . . oh, how I only wish I knew which Her we were talking about."

Elen stood there in the street, looking down at black eyes that seethed with intelligence the way Nina had said she seethed with sexuality, Kare's memory powering through her so strongly she could feel her, smell her, taste her. "I'm owned by my own stupidity," she said softly, still not able to confess. "Carpe diem, but I keep seizing the wrong one."

"Come to my house," Nina said quietly, "and let me tell you about a new course I'll be offering. It was your idea."

❏   ❏   ❏

"The Design of a Novel." Dr. Pinero smiled benignly at her Steinbeck class on the last day of the fall 1979 semester. "This essay by May Sarton I'm handing out is the core of a course I've convinced the president to allow me to inflict upon eight insane seniors in the spring 1981 semester. So why tell you now? I quote: 'A novel requires a long breath . . . It can, to some extent, be planned ahead over a considerable period of time. The seed may lie dormant for a long time, but little by little it magnetizes the imagination. It begins to *haunt.*' I tell you now that you might seek your seed, find it, begin to be haunted. Read this essay a hundred times before you sign up for this course—and don't sign up unless you're ready to write fifty thousand words—at two hundred and fifty words to the page, that's two hundred pages—you're willing to offer a publisher. You have three semesters to think. You won't be allowed to carry more than twelve hours in the semester you take the Novel course. You know my office hours. Have a good Christmas."

"Sign me up, Dr. P." Elen grinned, that lazy, razory grin of hers. "I've already read the essay a hundred times. Hell, I could be the new Audre Lourde, the new Rita Mae Brown, the new—"

"The new bullshit artist of the twenty-first century," grumbled the boy she had ragged about his daddy making his car payments. "You sure do think you're hot shit, McNally."

She laughed, a slow, easy amusement, her hazel eyes taunting him; he hated her almost as desperately as he wanted to get her into bed, and she knew it. "Ayuh, Jeff, I do. And I'd probably think you were just plain shit, if I ever wasted my time thinking about you at all."

"Queer bitch," he snarled, and simmered from the room; Elen shook her head. If he didn't remind her so much of Chuckie Cheeseballs—

"Someday he'll come back at you, Elen," she heard, and turned. "You really ride him hard."

"If he ever tries me, I'll ride his young ass hard and put it away wet, and not like he had in mind." She was in the middle of draping a lazy smile all over the shy and tiny woman who had spoken when she realized by the blue eyes looking up at her that she was facing one of the women Nina had said would sacrifice major body parts if she'd only approach them. "Excuse me," she said faintly, and turned and sneezed three times in violent succession. "God, I'm allergic to semester break. Quick, Dr. P.; give me something to read."

"You're on your own until Greek Lit," Nina grinned, gathering her papers. "But we'll open with the Iliad, if you're that horny to get started."

"Rosy-fingered dawn," Elen said weakly. "He fell thunderously, and his armor clattered upon him." She had read it already, on Kare's midnight advice.

"Yond Cassius," Nina said dryly, "has a lean and hungry look."

Elen barked a laugh as Nina headed for the door. "'If ever I say to the passing moment, "Linger a while! Thou art so fair!" then you may cast me into fetters; I will gladly perish then and there.'"

Nina stopped, and turned; her black eyes brimmed with amusement. "'Think what you're saying; we shall not forget it.'"

"'If I stay as I am, I am a slave,'" Elen drawled. "'Whether yours or another's, it's all the same.'"

Nina cackled in delight. "You told me you had good retention! The road to hell is paved with it, McNally, but Merry Christmas anyway. To Ms. Dana, I extend a more cordial holiday greeting."

Dana, mystified by the exchange, gave her a cautious smile. "You too, Dr. Pinero. I can't wait for Greek Lit."

Elen sneezed again. "I'm sorry; I must be coming down with something." Out in the hall, Nina snorted a laugh. "Piss off, Pinero," she muttered, and turned to be captured again by shy blue eyes. She saw that Dana Lake was strikingly attractive, not just fortyish pretty as she'd seemed before; nothing like a different light, she thought, and from somewhere words came before she could catch them, or even knew she was going to say them, accompanied by a smile that felt strange and new. "You've got beautiful eyes, Dana." *Christ, someone turn on the runway lights; I don't know if this is an approach or a crash landing.*

Dana looked away in warm confusion at the unexpected compliment, murmuring something that might have been a thank you.

"I'm sorry. That came out of nowhere" —Dana looked up again— "but it's true. Look, you want to go get a beer? Pinero'll probably be there. She's a hoot to drink with."

"I'd love to."

"Got a car, or do we walk?"

Dana reached for her jacket; Elen reached it first, and held it for her. "I walk, unless it's really cold. I just live down on Main Street." She looked up, hesitating only a moment before adding, "I've got beer there?"

Elen looked at her, unaware of the intensity of the look, or even, really, who she was looking at; it was Kare she saw, those green eyes just before the darkness when she had doused the candle to whisper, "Sometimes I wish you could look past Nikki far enough to see me."

Maybe it's time you thought about letting her go.

"Yes," she said softly. Almost unconsciously, she traced a thumb across Dana's cheekbone, her fingers barely touching soft ash-blonde hair. She could smell perfume, light as dust motes in a sunbeam, deep and velvety as the petals of a lover's rose; it occurred to her to begin at the tender sensitivity below Dana's ear and follow that scent wherever it led her. She caught herself as she started to bend her head, to reach for the willingness she saw in Dana's eyes. "I'm sorry," she murmured, but she didn't retreat; Dana couldn't seem to, either. Their eyes were still locked, searching. "Are you sure you want to take me home with you?"

"I haven't been so sure of anything for a long time."

❏   ❏   ❏

It was a short walk from the university to Dana's apartment, no more than six blocks; the air was crisp and cleared their heads. They didn't talk. When Dana would have started up the walk to her building, Elen touched her elbow. "Dana, if you'd rather go down to the restaurant—"

"I . . . no. Will you come up? I really do have some beer."

"Do you really have some scotch?" *Where the hell did that come from? Oh, Kare, were you a blessing or a curse, and what are you doing to me now?*

"Chivas Regal?"

Why am I not surprised? "My brand." She tackled Kare's memory, wrestling it to a closet in her mind, and stuffed it in and slammed the door as she followed Dana up the walk, up the stairs. "Neat," she said to a query of mix, draping her coat across a kitchen chair; the apartment was small, white-glove neat, feminine but not frilly. "Thanks." She accepted the drink; it was as smooth as she remembered, as smokily sweet as the scent of auburn hair on a hot Texas night. *Goddamnit, Kare, back off. You left me; now leave me alone. I like this woman.* "I like your place."

"It's a bitch to dust, living on Main Street." She gave Elen a nervous smile. "I've been in this dress since six this morning. I'm not offering to slip into something more comfortable, but—"

"But you refuse to spend another thirty seconds in panty hose," Elen grinned. "Work you late tonight, did they?" Dana usually wore jeans to class. Trim, tight jeans.

"I get so pissed," Dana said from the bedroom. "They know I've got a night class. I swear they don't want me to get this degree for fear they'll have to pay me more. Oh, damn—damn! Elen, help." She emerged barefoot but still in the dress. "Damn zipper. Is it stuck or broken?"

"Caught—oh, damn. Really caught." She put her drink down; the cigarette she had lit smoldered away in the ashtray while she tried to free the zipper without damaging the silk. Dana's perfume was soft in her scent; the back of her neck looked like an invitation. "There," she murmured at last, and eased the zipper the rest of the way down, but Dana didn't step away from her; Elen let her lips brush the curve of a

shoulder bared by the zipper's undoing, and felt the tiny
shiver that rippled through them both. She found Dana's waist
with her hands, bringing her back against her; this time her
lips more than brushed Dana's skin. "Anything else I can do?"
she asked softly.

"You are—" It was a whisper as Elen drew the tip of
her tongue from her shoulder to her neck, and to her ear;
gently, she closed her teeth on Dana's earlobe. "Elen, don't
stop—"

"I will if you tell me to." She knew there was nothing
under that black silk dress but a black silk slip. She slipped
her palms across Dana's belly to draw her closer; she grazed
her lips across her cheek, and found the corner of her mouth
with her tongue, and whispered there: "Tell me what you
want, Dana."

*I've never made love to a woman before, Kare . . . tell
me what you want.*

Dana felt a flicker, a catch of breath; she might have
asked about it, had she had time, but Elen was turning her,
finding her mouth with her own, her hands finding silk,
seeking skin, her tongue probing in delicate inquiry; when
Elen slipped the dress from her shoulders and helped it slither
to the floor, and moved her gently away from it, her hands
making palms against the thin silk slip, against her waist and
her back and her ribs, against her hair and her hips and her
face, she forgot the question. When Elen lifted her into her
arms and carried her to the bedroom, Dana forgot there had
been a question. Her only wonder was why, when she woke
at nine Friday morning, she found herself warmly, smoothly
naked with Elen McNally wrapped around her in a tangle of
arms and legs and breaths—in jeans and a washed-soft cotton
T-shirt.

"I don't know what's wrong," she hedged to the receptionist for Wentworth, Barrett & Logan, Attorneys at Law, as Elen's teeth raked across the rise of her hip while Dana tried without much seriousness or success to fend her off from her moistening goal, "but no will way I be in today. Jean, I've got to go—"

Jean hung up knowing damn well Dana had been—and was probably right now being—laid into blathering insensibility. "More power to you," she grinned, and told W, B and L that their executive secretary had the double-ended flu. If they wanted to take that as whoops and poops, good for them; to her it meant Friday and Monday.

❏   ❏   ❏

Her mother took one look at her and said, "Elen, you're using something, aren't you?" Elen saw the lack of accusation, the wealth of love and concern in her face, and she said softly, "Mom, believe me. I won't get pregnant." And somehow it didn't surprise her when her mother tapped gently on her bedroom door as she was dressing after her shower and came in to sit on the edge of her bed and finally look up and ask quietly, "Elen, are you gay?"

Slowly, Elen sat at her desk chair, resting her elbows on her knees and her head in her hands; she knotted her fingers in her hair. She'd figured her mother had an idea, but she'd never thought she would ask; she'd had her neat little speech all written, for when it was time to tell her, but until there was someone— "Yeah," she said softly. "Yeah, Mom. I am."

Elizabeth McNally closed her eyes; for a brief, wounded moment she sat there, and then she looked up, dry-eyed. "Anne?"

Anne had been her inseparable best friend in high school; Anne wouldn't speak to her now. So much for honesty between friends. "No. It's a short list until this weekend, Mom. Kare Dillinger."

"Maj—an officer, Elen?" It was a strange combination of horror and pride.

"Rank had nothing to do with us loving each other. We did, Mom. But it had everything to do with—she got transferred to Germany and I wouldn't re-up to go with her. I'd have wrecked her career and she's headed for a star—or two. We talked about my going over there when I got out, but—we wrote for a while, but—" She sat back in the chair, pushing through the clutter on her desk to find cigarettes and lighter. "But it's over," she said softly. "You know how long it's been since I got a letter from Germany."

"You still love her—?" It wasn't a question, precisely; more like just giving her the opportunity to deny it.

"I did love her. And I love that I loved her. I don't love that it didn't last, but I know it's over."

Looking at her daughter's eyes, Liz had her doubts about how over it was in Elen's heart. "Where does Nikki fit into all of this?" she asked quietly. "Somehow I get the feeling she's part of it."

Elen huffed a small, pained laugh. "I know as much about quantum physics as I know about where Nikki fits. Like a key in a lock? Put the key in, turn it, something opens; take the key out. Door's open but the key's gone. You can close it, but you can never lock it again. There's almost nothing about her that I understand, Mom—including why I still care so much about her."

"It's hard not to care about someone who made such a difference in your life," Liz said gently. "You don't stop loving a person just because they're gone from you, from Mrs. Violette in third grade, to Erin, to Nikki. To Kare."

Elen studied her mother for a moment, and finally gave a tiny shake of her head. "You're a trip, Mom," she murmured, and when she looked up again there was a different pain in her eyes. "Mama, how's Daddy going to take this?" She knew her father would be told.

"I'll tell him."

"Ayuh." She lit a cigarette and tossed her Zippo back to her desk, smoke hissing out between her teeth. "He won't kill you."

"He'll adjust," Liz said coolly, and somehow Elen didn't doubt that if Ezra McNally's attitude needed adjustment, Liz was the one who could wield the proper wrench— upside his head, if need be. "Give him time. Where will you be if I need to get in touch with you?"

Elen found a scrap of paper on her desk and wrote Dana's number there; she had only come home for a change of clothes. "Just ask for me."

Liz smoothed the slip of paper on her lap. "Will she make you happy, Elen?" Her voice was very soft; Elen looked up and saw tears glimmering.

"Mom, it's who I am," she said gently. "Happiness isn't guaranteed. If I was straight I might marry some jerk who beat me up." She reached to touch her mother's hand; Liz laced her fingers through her daughter's. "I'm sorry about grandchildren," Elen said softly, and Liz shook her head in silent protest, but couldn't keep the tears from spilling over. "You and Daddy would be such great grandparents, but Mom, I don't—I can't—see me as a mother."

"Elen, what did we do—" The rest of the question was a mute appeal.

"You didn't do anything. Mama, please believe that. I know Daddy's going to do this thing like, 'Oh, I taught her how to hunt and fish and shoot pool and change the oil in the

car and that's why she's gay.' Well, your dad taught you how
to hunt and fish and change the oil in the car, too, and you're
not gay, and I can't see that learning how to shoot pool made
the difference. Mom—" She let go of her mother's hand and
leaned back, and ran a hand through her still-damp hair and
fumbled another cigarette from her pack. "I never told you
this before because I didn't see any reason to, but I got raped
down at—Mom, don't cry. Please. It happened, and I cried,
and when I was done crying it'd still happened. He hurt me
and Nikki healed me. Nikki hurt me and Kare healed me.
Nothing you or Daddy did made me a lesbian, and Jesus,
please don't think you failed. Mama, it'd hurt so bad to know
you thought that. I still need for you to be proud of me. I still
need you to love me—"

"You're my daughter, Elen Mary, and I'll love you until
I die and after that. And I am proud of you, but—"

"But?" Elen looked at her. "But don't buy you any
T-shirts that say, my daughter's gay and that's okay, huh?
'But' is just as bad as 'where did we go wrong.' Ma, I spent
all of junior high and high school with guys laughing at me
because I was fat. I spent my first three months at Hood trying
to make up for it—I slept around a lot," she said almost coldly,
to her mother's cautiously questioning look. "I'm sorry. You
can't believe how sorry I am for it, because it gave this one
guy the idea that I was a free shot. Well, I wasn't. No woman
is, no matter what she's done before. He hurt my body, he
hurt my pride, he hurt everything female and everything
human in me, and as bad as Nikki hurt me and as bad as Kare
hurt me, they didn't even come close to what he did to me.
And I've got other dykes gnarling with me about this all the
time; they've got this big debate going about whether it's
environmental or genetic and how no one chooses to be gay,
but I chose. I chose. They can call it environmental if they

want to, but the way I see it, I was strong enough to make a decision I damnwell knew wouldn't be popular. If you need to take responsibility for something, take it for having raised me to have an open mind, because once I really opened my mind to it, there was nothing wrong with the idea of two women making love."

Liz almost flinched; Elen sat forward again. "Mom, you taught me it was all right to masturbate," she said gently. "You said it was natural, that it was how people learn about sexuality. What do I do when I masturbate, except make love to a woman? Am I really embarrassing you, Mom? I want you to understand, but I don't want to hurt you."

"Elen—baby, it doesn't hurt," she whispered. "It's just so different. I never had to think this way. I never had to look at these ideas."

"You must have. You asked me if I was gay."

"But I didn't look at it this—this closely, Elen." Her laugh was small and shaky. "You have to admit this is a pretty close look, honey, what you're talking about."

"I know. Maybe I shouldn't have gone this deep into it, but Mama, I don't want you to think what I'm doing is bad, because it isn't. There's nothing perverse or sick or evil about it, or me, or the woman I spent the night with."

"May I ask who?"

"Dana Lake." She smiled at the shock in her mother's eyes; WB&L was, and had been for years, their law firm. "Surprised? You never know who we might be, Mom. Ten percent of the world is homosexual—and ninety percent of the gay population are so deep in the closet they've got coat hangers growing out their backs. 'But that I were forbid to tell the secrets of my prison-house, I could a tale unfold whose lightest word would harrow up thy soul . . .' You wouldn't believe who's gay in this town."

"I don't want to know," her mother whispered.

"I wouldn't tell you. It's your business that I'm gay, but not that Mr. X or Ms. Y are. I'm just saying it happens in the best of families, and there's a lot of people who'll never look at you funny because you've got a gay kid. And it isn't that I broadcast it, Mom, but I don't try to hide, either. And if the next question is 'will I ever go back to men,' I guess I'd rather drink a pint of kerosene and piss on a brush fire than even consider it. I'm here. I'm gay."

Liz stood. "You picked up some of the most disgusting expressions while you were in the Army." She bent to give her only surviving child a kiss on the top of her damp head. "I love you, Elen. And I'll talk to your father."

"I feel like such a wimp, asking you to do that for me."

"He wouldn't kill you, honey. But he won't try to talk me out of it."

CHAPTER THIRTEEN

"So do we have plans for tonight?" Elen lazed naked across Dana's bed in the bright afternoon light, eating grapes off the stem and watching through the bathroom door as Dana shaved her legs on the edge of the tub. "New Year's Eve and all. Damn, you make that look like fun. You sure you don't need help?"

Dana glinted a smile at her. "I'll manage, thanks." She took a last stroke with the razor and rinsed it off under the tap. "Did you shave all your other lovers' legs for them?"

Elen flipped the empty grape stem into the wastebasket by the bed. "You make it sound like there's been so many." She sat up, finding her shirt from yesterday, tugging it on.

"Well, it's fairly obvious."

"Don't assume. You know what happens." She stepped into her jeans. "Makes an ass out of you and me."

"Get snippy, why don't you." She ran a washcloth over her legs and slipped into her robe. "No one gets as good in bed as you are without practice, Elen."

"I didn't mean to be snippy—but it doesn't take two to practice."

Dana snorted a laugh. "Sure. Like you were a virgin when you met me."

"In a way, I was," Elen murmured. "In a way, I still am."

"What the hell is that supposed to mean?"

I knew there wasn't going to be any easy way around this. "Dana, don't be defensive. Please. We just need to talk about this. It's a problem for me."

"I don't even know what you're talking about."

Elen leaned wearily against the dresser. There was an unpleasant edge in Dana's voice; it wasn't the first time in the last two weeks that it had been there. "Have you ever touched me, Dana?" Softly, she asked, not knowing any way but the shortest distance between two points. *I probably couldn't let you if you tried, but you could at least try.* "This is feeling a little one-sided."

"You bitch!"

"Dana, please. I don't want to fight. Can't we just talk about it?"

"You're the one who came on to me. You're always the one to initiate sex. I let you even when I don't feel like—"

"Dana, that's crazy! Christ, I can get laid anytime I want to. That's not why I'm here, honey, I want us to—"

"Well, excuse me for holding you back! Go! Get laid! Fuck the whole phys ed department if you want to!"

"Dana—" She reached for her. "Dana, I didn't mean it that way; god, you know I didn't. Honey, pleas—"

Dana slapped her, a hard, brutally angry slap that rocked her back on her heels, stumbling her back two steps; she reached in speechless amazement for her face. There was a weird, slant-lit suspension of space and time, like a photograph or a painting, before Dana whispered huge-eyed, "Elen, I'm sorry—"

"No," Elen said softly. "No, Dana. Goodbye." Her backpack was on the cedar chest at the end of the bed; she caught it on her way by and went through the apartment like a predator, her prey anything of her own; behind her, Dana wept apologies. She paused at the door. "Don't call me, Dana," she said with cold, gentle finality. "Don't even bother to think about it."

She went home and took a steaming shower, using Lava and loofah. "I'm fine," she snapped at her mother, when that perceptive woman asked gently if she was all right, and Liz gave her a look that suggested if her daughter was fine, her daughter's mother was the Queen of England, and Elen said, "Oh, god, Mama, I'm sorry—" and collapsed into her arms and wept, wondering if this was the only woman who would ever love her enough not to tear her heart to pieces. Once she was cried out she was embarrassed; she laced up her sneakers and charged out of the house to run. It was warm, the snow melting sloppily; she splashed through rivulets of water, soaking herself to the knees in the first of four miles she ate with her long stride. By the time she got back to the head of the street she was clearheaded; nothing like a good cry, a long run, and knowing without question that—and why—it was over. She walked the last two blocks, cooling down, and shed her sweats in the bathroom and took a gentler shower, and pulled on faded fatigue pants and a T-shirt from the Fifth First Annual Intergalactic Oatmeal Cookoff and Bertram Acceleration Day; Oatmeal & Bertram, Texas; she and Kare had gone. Kare had a shirt, too. "Mail for you, honey," her mother said, when she wandered to the kitchen in search of something to eat. "On the dining room table. Do you feel better?"

"Yeah, I'm okay. She slapped me," she said, and Liz looked up sharply. "Hey, no harm, no foul. I could've fallen in love. I thought I had, actually, but I sure fell out quick. Nothing like a little domestic violence. As it is, I got the edge taken off my libido; that's something, I guess."

"Elen Mary, that's crude."

"Hitting me was pretty damned crude. Am I supposed to respect her?" She ran a finger into the bowl of cookie batter her mother was mixing. "Is Daddy ever going to talk to me again?"

"You know how he needs to work up to things. He'll get to it. Did I tell you you had a package?"

Elen pushed away from the counter, sucking raw cookie from her finger; she found a small box on the dining room table and turned it so she could see the return address. "Provincetown, Massachusetts?" She opened her pocketknife and slit the tape. "I don't know anyone in P'town."

She opened the end of the box and peeked in, and drew out a soft wad of tissue paper, squeezing to feel some small, hard thing; she opened it to find a shell—or, part of a shell, the remains of a shell. It had been a tiny conch, perhaps three inches long had it been intact, but sometime long ago it had been broken, and had tumbled in the sea for however long it had taken to soften and gentle it, to expose its inner intricacy in a graceful delicacy of soft pinks and whites; it was broken, but beautiful, and she looked at it in bewilderment. "What the—?" She looked back into the box. There was more tissue paper; she drew it out. This piece was heavy, taped together; she opened her knife again.

Two perfect alabaster eggs, smooth and cool in her hands, as pale a cream as the inside of the fragment of shell.

famous one egg omelet except I used two—

"What did you get, honey?" her mother asked from the doorway.

"I don't know," she said slowly, looking at the eggs, and the poignant piece of shell. She tipped the box so she could look in; there was more tissue in the bottom. She reached for it.

Nestled in the paper was the wire bail and ceramic stopper of a Grolsch bottle. "Oh, god," she whispered. "Nikki—"

Liz turned. Silently, she pulled the door behind her.

Elen didn't hear. There was an envelope in the bottom of the box.

It was Henry. I found all your letters, Elen, and the ones I wrote to you while I stayed with him. I gave up a long time before you did. I'm so sorry.

These things screamed your memory at me when I found them. I've had them a long time, meaning them for you, but it wasn't until I knew what he did to us that I dared to send them.

I think of you so often—I wonder how and who you are now, and if you ever became who I thought you would be. I still wish I'd been strong enough, not just to be your friend but to give you the time that was all you needed, if I was right. But I was losing it and I couldn't take the chance on taking you down with me. I did love you, Elen. I still do.

It was a long climb back up, but the view's great at the top. If you're ever in the valley with mountains on every side of you, know it can be done. And if you ever need me, I'm still yours, Nikki

❏   ❏   ❏

"Goddamn it, Elen, that's enough!" Ezra McNally heard one too many cabinet doors bang sharply shut; he launched from his chair with a roar. "You've been god-damned impossible to live with for a week! You'd better get your head out of your ass, little girl, or you can find another place to live, and don't think I don't mean it! I won't have you slamming doors and snarling at your mother and me and—"

"Ezra," Liz said, the way wives do to let their husbands know what thin ice they're on, a cold and gentle tone that says, enough. It had always worked; it worked again.

But Elen didn't hear her, didn't know he had been curbed; she wheeled at him in fury. "You don't know a fucking thing about me! You don't know who I am or care if I hurt, and you might have spawned me but you don't own me, you son of a bitch, so take a good look at my back because I'm gone!"

"God damn you, you—"

"Ezra!" That was no cold and gentle tone; that was a whip that had never cracked before and it froze him two steps into following his daughter, and he felt of his own presence and realized his fist was closed and raised, and his stomach lurched in the realization that he had meant to hurt her.

"Sit down." Her voice wasn't the crack of the whip, this time, but the leather of it, brushing him in deadly warning, and he sank to the sofa and put his face in his hands, and he sat shivering, swallowing, subdued.

"Don't even try," Elen said through her teeth when her mother came into her room without knocking. "Save your breath. I'm out of here."

"I'm not going to ask you to apologize to your father," Liz said, as if Elen hadn't spoken and wasn't jamming clothes into her duffle bag. "What you said was cruel, but he drove you to it. He does love you, Elen, but he's hurt and confused and doesn't understand who you are or why you are, that much was right, but he does care. He does love you. And if you leave now, you might never be able to make it right between you because you'll both carry that anger and hurt around with you, blaming each other. And if you leave, Elen, it's going to damage our marriage, because I'll blame him for driving you away. That may sound like more responsibility than you deserve, but it's the truth. I can do a lot, but I can't subjugate the ego of a man. If you leave in the morning, he'll let you come back. If you leave now, he never will. So you think about what you want, and you think about what you can live with—tonight, and for the rest of your life." She turned from the room, closing the door quietly behind her, and stopped in the hallway, halfway between all she loved, and she closed her eyes and felt the deep thrum of panic trying to start in her, and she clamped her jaw and fought her own fight until the panic crept defeated away from her. She went back to the living room.

"If you ever lay a hand on her in anger," she said to Ezra's back, for he was staring out the window into the night, "I'll divorce you. Now come to bed."

None of them slept that night, but they did it under the same roof. In the early morning they gave up and got up and edged around each other in the kitchen, drinking coffee, until finally Elen said, "It's a week before classes start. I think I'll drive down to the Cape."

Silence.

Finally, rough and reluctant: "You got enough money?"

"Yeah." And a long moment later, "But thanks."

❏   ❏   ❏

But she didn't go to the Cape; she couldn't find the courage to get any farther south than Camden. She took a cheap off-season room with a view of the grey winter harbor and huddled there with a carton of cigarettes and a half- gallon of vodka and a notebook, trying to figure out who she loved, or if she loved, or if she did, why she did, and drove home Sunday without having called Nikki, knowing only that the haunting of which the great writer had spoken had begun.

CHAPTER FOURTEEN

Nina Pinero watched from under the brim of a ragged old Australian bush hat as Elen slid on her back under her Celica until all that showed of her were feet clad in a pair of ankle-high work boots that made both the car and Nina's hat look pristine and new. "Son of a whore. He's right," came her voice; momentarily most of the exhaust system of the car appeared, a pipe here and a muffler there, some of it disintegrating into rust flakes when it hit the ground. Nina tipped back her beer, grinning at Elen's feet. Elen was an aristocrat without a horse, set afoot by the inspection station until the muffler was replaced, poor enough to eschew the station's offer of repair; she bought parts Friday afternoon and was investing her time Saturday to install them. Her mother's car was also parked in Nina's driveway; she used it twice to go to the parts store. Two hours later she fired up the Celica for a critical listen. Satisfied, she accepted the cold beer Nina offered and sat with the professor on the back steps, shaking her head; flakes of rust and road dirt sifted from her hair. Her hands were black with grime, her face smudged with it, her T-shirt a disaster. She was bleeding from several knuckles, but had long forgotten that fact.

"Have you called Nikki?" Quietly, Nina asked; it was an occasional question of hers.

Elen glanced at her. "Yeah," she said at last. "Yeah. I did."

"And?"

She drizzled beer over the bleeders on her right hand. "We talked. Caught up on our lives. She's cooking in a restaurant in P'town. Loves it."

"When will you see her?"

Elen tipped her beer, taking the rest of it in a swallow. "Sometime," she said softly. "That's what we said, after saying nothing for twenty minutes: we should get together sometime. Like she's got any other reason but me to come here, or I've got any reason but her to go there, and neither one of us've got reason enough. Old Army buddies. We'll run into each other someday and have a bunch of beers and reminisce about the old days.

"They say you fall in love?" Her laugh was brief, bitter. "You trip into it, and skin your heart, and it hurts and then it scabs over, and you pick the scab a couple of times and it keeps hurting, but after a while it heals and all you've got is a scar you notice every now and then to remember how you got it. I think all I really wanted was to know she was all right. Now I know. She only wanted to know if she was right about me. Now she knows. What's left?"

"Do you regret the time you spent caring about her?"

Elen looked at her. "'Deep as first love, and wild with all regret; O Death in Life, the days that are no more,'" she said softly. "Tennyson."

Nina got up and went into the kitchen for a fresh pair of beers, coming back to find Elen in a reflective sprawl on the steps. "What nature is it you contemplate now?" she asked, passing Elen the new cold beer.

"Memory," Elen said slowly. "It's funny, what you'll remember." She tasted her beer, and picked at the label.

"Before I went in the service I went to visit the aunts—they're like, eighty and eighty-five? Neat old ladies. They had this screen house out in the back yard so they could sit in the evenings without getting carried off by the mosquitos? We were sitting out there having a drink one afternoon and I heard a noise—it sounded like a junebug on the back door, you know how they'll buzz along the screen trying to get at the light? I got up to look, and there was a hummingbird stuck in the screen. It was that light fiberglass screening—I don't know what hummingbirds have for eyesight, but I guess she'd just been zooming along and crashed right into it, and she'd jammed her beak into the mesh and couldn't get out. She was trying to fly backwards, trying to pull herself out, and that was what I'd heard, the sound of her wings beating against the screen—beating against herself. She was beating herself to death, trying to get free."

The look in her eyes was familiar; the professor had seen it dozens of times in class when she'd said "Write" and Elen had uncapped that bold Waterman pen: it was that gathering look, gazing past time to see the thing again.

"First I tried to push her out from the inside. I figured I could just pop her out, but she was really stuck. They fly forty, fifty miles an hour, you know? so if she was booking it for home, she might have been going top end when she hit. Christ, what a shock that must have been, fetching up so short." She shook her head. "When I saw it wouldn't be that easy I really looked, and I could see there was a covering, like a skin but harder, on her beak and that was—peeling back, from her trying to get loose, and if I pushed the way I'd done at first I was going to really hurt her. I had one of those Swiss Army knives with the little scissors on it—I cut the screen so I could get one hand out to hold her while I got those scissors positioned so I could cut the hole she was stuck in without amputating her beak. God, it was careful work, and I'd had two drinks, and she was—she was the most fragile—the most vibrant thing I've ever held in my hand."

Elen talked with her hands, and Nina watched the absorbing delicacy of the rescue in those long, gentle fingers; she saw the hummingbird restrained there with aching tenderness, those fingers afraid of doing harm to the tiny vulnerability they held, and the trepidation in the hand holding a tool not designed for such delicate surgery. She glanced up at the expressive hazel eyes; they didn't fit the tale, so filled were they with a bewildered disquiet.

"One of the aunts got some peroxide from the house and we put a drop of it on her beak—she was bleeding—and I opened my hands—and except for a slit in the screen and the memory, it was as if she'd never been there. That was five years ago, and I still remember how she felt in my hand. She didn't struggle, she . . . pulsed. It was almost like she knew I was all that could save her, and she had to trust me. She had no reason to. She just did. What I felt wasn't her life, but her desperation."

Nina waited. They drank. Elen lit a cigarette, and the soft, warm June breeze carried the smoke away.

"I remember the look in her eyes when she said 'sometimes I—' and someone yelled for her and that was it—but that look was like an echo in me," Elen said softly, and Nina, who had sensed all along that nothing was really about Nikki, sensed that this wasn't, either. "I remember how she looked, across the candle from me that night out in the field. I remember how she smelled—sweat, and Chanel Number Five." She shivered, remembering. "It was hot—god, it was hot. But her nipples were hard. I remember wondering why."

Silently, Nina drew a tiny clay pipe from her pocket. She packed it and lit it, and the soft, warm June breeze carried the smoke away.

"And then she asked for me." Elen leaned forward with a soft sigh, her elbows on her knees; she traced a finger along a small, thin scar on her forehead. "I remember how it felt when she touched me—just her fingers against my throat, against the back of my neck—the way I remember how small the space a hummingbird took in my hand, and the sound of it when I opened my fingers and it understood it was free." Her tongue made a soft fluttering sound. "She exploded in my hand, so desperate for freedom—" Her voice was low, rich, deeply vibrant. "I held her—I heard her voice through her body, and she sounded like that hummingbird—but like she'd flown past the danger and found a flower to sip, instead of impaling herself on something she hadn't even known was there. She sounded like life, and reason, and healing. And me . . . I felt like a bird with my beak caught in a screen, pulsing in her custody while she cut it away." She took a last hot taste of her cigarette and fired the butt into the driveway. It smoldered there; the soft, warm June breeze carried the smoke away. "Why didn't it happen? Why am I still caught in the screen?"

"Where is your hummingbird now?"

For a long time Elen didn't speak, or move. "Caught in some other screen," she said at last; her voice was soft and resigned. "The one we pull around ourselves at night to keep the things that fly in the dark away from us."

❏   ❏   ❏

"Oh goddamn it all to hell, you'd think as many times as you'd done this you'd know it comes out at an angle,

McNally, you Christless moron. Jesus Harley-Davidson
Christ in a sidecar—"

Ezra McNally listened to his daughter under her rag-
gedy old Toyota, and had a cloth ready for her when she
skidded out from under on a creeper, oil on her face. "Christ.
Thanks." She mopped at the oil, spitting into the rag; of course
she'd had her mouth open. Disgusted, she wiped her hands.
She was getting tired of trying to hold the heap together with
baling wire and bubble gum, but neither was she ready for a
new set of car payments. Her father offered a beer. She
accepted. "What's all this?"

"What's all what?"

She couldn't help it. "You, acting like you know me."
Since their blowup they had edged around each other like
dogs overlapping the borders of their piss zones, coexisting
but cautious, with a snarl or a snap now and then; this was
August, and until now he hadn't offered cold beers on hot
days, or hunkered down in the driveway with her. They hadn't
shot a game of pool together, or gone snowmobiling when
there was snow, or fishing when the ice went out. But here
was a beer and a hunker, and a look in his eyes that said
something was wrong; she saw that, on second glance. "What,
Dad?" And when he looked at her and away again in tight-
lipped misery, she didn't want to know. "Daddy—?"

"The story on the news last night about the woman they
found in Cambridge? The one someone beat to death because—" He stopped, and cleared his throat.

"Because she was a lesbian. They call it gay-bashing,
Dad." The story had enraged her: the anchorman's tone of
voice, the slippery implications of his expression and his body
language, how long the camera had lingered on the blood-
stained sidewalk and the spray-painted wall: *queers die*, as if
it was a suggestion, not an obscenity.

"They've identified her," he said quietly. "Honey, it was Nikki Cole."

He saw it hit her, a jolt like grabbing both parts of a live wire.

"No—" She sagged against the car, her head meeting the door with a thump, her breath caught in her; foggily, she wondered if it showed, that feeling that someone had just driven the end of a ball bat into the small of her back; she wondered if he could see how her heart had just turned to ice. "Oh. God. No."

It showed. He had spent the last months fighting feelings that raged from towering anger to love so helpless it made him weep for what he was doing to her, but that familiar name on the noon newscast had made his heart stumble in his chest, a flutter of fear that whispered *Nikki that's Elen's Nikki and Elen could have been with her—it could have been Elen and for no other reason than that? How can someone kill someone for no more reason than that?* And sickly, he knew that was what he was doing to her heart, for no more reason than that.

He touched her knee and she looked it him in mute, stunned appeal: for it not to be true, or if it was, for him to forget for a moment that he didn't love her anymore (he saw that in her eyes, and it felt like dying himself), for him to be Daddy to his little girl again and hold her. He took her against him, but she didn't cry; she just shivered in the thick August heat, and for a long time they sat that way, a sixty-year-old man feeling twice as old, holding his daughter on his lap, trying to absorb some of her pain. "I'm sorry, baby," he whispered, for Nikki and a lot of other things. "Elen, I'm so sorry."

"Daddy, she can't—oh, Daddy, no! I loved her, she can't be—"

"I know. I know, honey. I love you so much, baby—"
He couldn't remember the last time he had said it.

"Oh, Daddy—" And then she cried.

He had been afraid she wouldn't: not that she wouldn't
feel the pain, but that she wouldn't let it go. When Erin had
died, Elen hadn't cried, or if she had, she had done it alone—
*How would you know? You were so caught in your own pain
you didn't have time for her. That's your habit with her, isn't
it? That could've been your little girl on that sidewalk, dead
without knowing you love her, and crying on her casket
wouldn't have told her a thing. How many daughters do you
need to bury before you understand?*

"You be who you are," he whispered into her hair. "Be
gay or be straight, baby, but know I love you."

❏   ❏   ❏

"I'm okay, Dad. Really." Her voice sounded like an
echo in her own ears; she knew he didn't believe her, and
knew he was right not to. "I just need to be alone for a while."
Gently, she closed her bedroom door against him, and with
her hand still on the cool doorknob she rested her forehead
against the wood and tried to crowd back a new wave of tears,
but they overpowered her; the pain lodged in her chest felt
like she had swallowed too much of something too cold, too
fast. She turned, groping for her desk chair, and sank into it,
and she found the broken, tide-smoothed shell Nikki had sent
her and pressed it to her lips like a seal to keep the scream of
rage inside: what in hell were you thinking, leaving a dyke
bar and walking home alone at midnight? Didn't you know-
they'd be out there? Jesus, Nikki, you're—you were—oh
Jesus past tense Nikki why? You're smarter than that, you're
supposed to be there, you said if I ever needed you and now

you're past tense? No! Nikki, no, I need you now, don't be dead goddamn it Nikki don't be

At last she could sit back; with the shell still squeezed in her hand she glared at the ceiling, her jaw clenched so hard her teeth ached; she focused on that, willing the tears to stop. They slowed, and a sigh shivered from her. "Oh, Nikki," she whispered, and just her name spoken aloud thudded that icy ache back into her; she waited it out, her breath shallow and painful in her, the shell hard and smooth and warm in her hand.

She reached for her cigarettes, and fumbled one from the pack. She held it for a long moment, and caught herself getting that fragment of shell into position in her hand to strike the light; she jittered a laugh and put the shell down and spun the wheel on her Zippo. It sputtered, out of fluid. She threw it and the cigarette to her desk. Trembling, she drew her hands over her face; leaning her elbows onto her knees, she rested there in numbed exhaustion.

Nikki. Oh, god, Nikki, why? We never even had that beer.

She fingered a photo album from her bookshelf. Slowly, she turned pages: Nikki at the lake, overdressed against the Texas sun. Nikki on her bed in the Haven, a book in one hand, one finger of the other offering good-natured sign language. Nikki on mess duty out in the field, offering a ladle full of something memorably inedible (liver stew) to the Executive Officer—

Kare.

She snapped the album shut, but it was too late; memory penetrated her, filled her, impaled her on an ache of loss, of missing her, of needing her—for all through losing Nikki the first time, it had been Kare who had been there for her, and now— Kare had known her, understood her; Kare would know how to ease the pain again. She fumbled for her address book, for the only entry under D, and she reached for the phone, but when the operator asked how he could help her she sat suspended, Germany on the tip of her tongue and a year of silence on the tip of her heart, until he asked again. "Never mind," she said roughly. "Sorry."

She found her cigarettes and pushed through a desk drawer for matches. She smoked, shivering, freezing in the August afternoon. She stubbed out the cigarette, chasing embers around the ashtray until they were dead.

She paged slowly through her address book, seeking someone else who had known them, her and Nikki.

Bill Buckman? A hollow smile twitched to her, there and gone. Christmas cards to him had gone unanswered; the Oscar for *Punchline* brooded on her desk, a naked, sexless shaft of conflicting memories.

Luke Czosnik? She had called him a few times, and he her a few times; all they had in common anymore was a tendency to drink too much every now and then and ride the phone wires in pursuit of old Army buddies. She tried to imagine what she might say to Luke about Nikki, and turned the page.

Tight-lipped, she flipped past D.

Jeannie Kincaid?

"The number you have reached is no longer in service. Please check . . ."

"Shit, Jeannie! You might've sent a postcard, you know?"

There was no one else between those covers who had known her.

She turned back to Kare's page, and touched her name with a finger; she sighed. Gently, she closed the book. She stood, feeling as stiff and sore as the bones of old women, and

went to find her father staring blankly at a television that
wasn't on. "Hey," she said softly. Hollow-eyed, he looked
up. "You think maybe we could go fishing?"

❑   ❑   ❑

They went to Deboullie Pond, where Nikki had told her
she had once gone. They caught a lot of trout, releasing most
of them, eating some of them; they talked. They talked in the
canoe, they talked around their tiny campfire, they talked half
the night, making up for ten years of virtual silence. Some of
it was painful for Elen; almost all of it was painful for Ezra,
but by the time they were ready to strike their tent and brave
the rough road out he was proud of his daughter again, and
knew how terribly he had missed that—and that the missing
had been his own hardheaded fault. As they pulled into the
driveway, tired and ripe from four days without more bath
than a swim in a deep glacier-cut pond, Elen said, "Now take
Mom somewhere. Talk to her like you talked to me. Listen to
her like you listened to me. You guys need to get well, too."
        "It doesn't seem like a very good time to leave you all
alone, baby."
        "Being alone is easy. It's being lonely that's hard, Dad,
and I think Mom misses you. I think you miss her. Go to
Bermuda or somewhere. Walk on the beach. Fall in love
again."
        He studied her for a moment, and finally got out of the
truck. "Leave that," he said, when she started to unload their
gear. "Will you do something for me while we're gone?"
        She followed him into the house. "What's that?"
        He went to his desk and bent there for a moment,
writing, and stood to offer a check. She looked, and looked
again in amazement at the numbers. "Go get yourself some

decent wheels," he said gruffly. "Get that rambling wreck of
yours out of my driveway."

"But Dad, I—this is a loan, right?"

"It's college money that I didn't have to spend. Oh, shut
up," he said crossly, when she started to protest. "Let's go
unload the truck."

CHAPTER FIFTEEN

"Literature: The Female Perspective; Pinero," Elen wrote, and browsed the rest of the page of the new university catalog. "American Playwrights: Albee, O'Neill and Williams; Pinero. Christ, she'll never let me get away with this. What's my core?" She thumbed pages back. "Physics? Fuck that this semester; my head ain't even right for it. Let's try—yeah, come in, Mom." There were two sets of knuckles that knocked on her door; this set was Liz. "Hi. What's up?"

"The mail came." Liz offered a fat envelope, tilted just enough that she couldn't see the hand, or the postmark.

Elen looked at it, and at her tight-lipped mother, and her stomach gave an uneasy twitch; the emotional tightrope she'd been walking in the three weeks since Nikki's death seemed suddenly thin as a blade. *Death and bad luck; it always runs in threes.* "How bad do I not want this?"

"I don't know, honey. It came."

Elen reached for it, but didn't look at it; she waited for Liz to close the door behind her before she turned the envelope in her hands. "Oh—" Liz heard that tiny oof of pain, and closed her eyes in that hardness of mothers' suffering for their children; she knew who the letter was from, and had debated for an hour before bringing it to Elen instead of burying it in the trash.

156

The hand was achingly familiar, the postmark German. "Oh, god. Kare—"

Liz heard that, too, but she had made her decision; the least she could do now was allow Elen privacy. She went down the hall, hugging herself.

I know it's been a long time, Elen. Maybe too long. There's no reason to believe you give a tinker's damn about any of what follows, but I need to say it. I haven't been able to get you off my mind for weeks. If you don't want to hear it, call it a ghost and give it the old heave-ho into the woodstove. If I don't hear from you, I'll stop haunting you. If you're with someone now, please be happy, please let her make love to you, and please don't read the rest of this. Leave me my pride, and burn it now.

"The hell and too late for you to stop haunting me," Elen muttered. Burning the letter was not an option.

I got the silver leaves on the first list. I've spent the last two years as a Brigade operations officer (and did I wish for a certain Ops Clerk I know). Now come job offers: Pentagon, a battalion command at McClellan, or a teaching position at the Command and General Staff College. Time to choose the rest of my life.

The Pentagon and the command are almost interchangeable. If I want the star, I have to have them both; it's only a matter of which one I'd rather do first. As far as CGSC goes — it's a plum in its own right, but 'Those who can, do' and all that. I've spent half my life waiting for this moment. Now here it is and I don't know what to do. I never thought there'd be a question. I'm scared, Elen. All I want is someplace calm and quiet. That isn't the Pentagon, or command of a training battalion. God, I wish you were here! You're the purest moment of sanity I ever had in my life; I was sane because of you. You gave me a balancing point. I've never wished for anything as much as I wish you were with me.

"Kare, don't do this to me," she whispered. "Please don't do this to me." But she read:

Turning forty was hard. It isn't that I feel old; it's just a milestone I ran into head-on, as if I never suspected it'd be there. I'm precisely where I thought I wanted to be, finding out that it isn't such a shit-hot place after all; did I assume all that time that I could be happy alone?

Elen dropped the pages to her desk. "Mary, Joseph, and Jesus," she whispered, her head in her hands, and finally she got up and went to the kitchen to make a drink: scotch neat. It wasn't yet noon. She knew by her mother's eyes that Liz was stretched on a hard rack between knowing Elen loved or had loved or would again love Kare, and hating her herself for having put a drink in her daughter's hand at eleven-fifteen in the morning. "She hurts, Ma," she said softly. "I'm not through it yet. I just know she's hurting." She took the drink back down the hall.

The warm scotch surged memories into her: lush hair and willingness, sweat and Chanel Number Five; the first woman's lips to open hungrily under hers, the first woman's nipple in her mouth since she was weaned, the first woman's wetness under her hand besides her own. "Oh, Kare," she whispered. She ran a shaky hand over her hair and turned the next page of the letter.

I asked too much, Elen, asking you to re-up. Your way was the only way, for your sanity and my survival. I couldn't see that for so long; when I did I still wouldn't admit I had been or was still wrong—I was wrong. I've been angry and hurt and lonely and I blamed it all on you. That's why I didn't write. Then forty came and I went to Austria, and spent a week in some stupid chalet and all I did was drink and cry and think about you—miss you—realize how much I still love and want and need you. I put my need for career success ahead of either of our lives, or any life we could have had together, when I knew you were the best thing that had happened or ever would happen to me. Now I have to choose and I can't, because what I want isn't on the list. So it comes down to this: Picture one five foot eleven redhead (one forty-two and holding with effort, but going slightly grey now), on her knees asking you to forgive her. Really see it, Elen; I mean it. I want you back. They can take their star and shove it.

"No, Goddess," Elen whispered. "Don't you go on your knees. Not for me. Not for anyone."

I trusted you to not read this if you're in a relationship; if you have, I'm trusting you're not. If you're willing to give me another chance (why should you? I sound crazier than a pet coon) I've got six weeks of leave; any or all of it for you. Tell me where you want to go. Anywhere, Elen. I'll send you tickets and meet you there.
This is how you always made me feel. I'd give anything to feel it again.

As I look at you my voice fails, my tongue is broken
and thin fire runs like a thief through my body.
My eyes are dead to light, my ears pound, and sweat
pours over me. I shudder, I am paler than grass.
—Sappho

❏   ❏   ❏

THIN FIRE RUNS LIKE A THIEF STOP DON'T GIVE ANYTHING JUST COME TO US AIRPORT PQI ASAP STOP PLAN ON ALL SIX CALM AND QUIET STOP THAT'S AN ORDER STOP THANK YOU THANK YOU THANK YOU GODDESS STOP ELLIOT NESS

❏   ❏   ❏

WILL ARRIVE PQI 0925 9 SEP STOP ALL SIX PLANNED STOP SCARED OUT OF MY WITS STOP THANK YOU THANK YOU THANK YOU TOO SQUIRT STOP CARPE DIEM STOP SAPPHO

BOOK THREE: KARE

CHAPTER SIXTEEN

"Excuse me, ma'am?" The captain had been told to look for a tall, beautiful redhead, and the only passenger on Bar Harbor flight 182 who fit that description was certainly tall and unquestionably beautiful, even if that hair might better be classified as—oh, auburn, maybe, or chestnut, or cinnamon— cinnamon, he decided (and a little bit of sugar, like on toast with too much butter when he was a kid); she looked up with a cautious half-smile. He gave back a grin. "They said tall and beautiful. You've been understated." He offered a long white box; she regarded it and him with undisguised mistrust. He held up a placating hand, seeing on second glance that she was as bone-tired as she was beautiful, and probably in no mood for flirtation however harmless. "I'm just a courier, ma'am. This is from someone in Presque Isle who's missed you awful bad. There's champagne to go with it when we're in the air."

She relented, accepting the box; he was handsome and harmless. "Thank you, Captain. For the delivery and the compliment." Only one thing came in a box like this; the only question was how many and what color. She waited for his last smile before he drew the cockpit curtain behind him, and lifted the lid.

The color of old burgundy wine, a single long-stemmed rose nestled in a froth of forget-me-nots. "Oh, Elen—" There was a card; she had to search her pockets for a tissue before she could read it.

Linger a while: Thou art so fair.

She lifted the rose from the box and touched it to her lips, and dissolved into quiet tears; the stewardess came with the champagne, and saw the rose and the tears and came back with ice and a cloth for when they were needed. She drank all of the champagne, trying to knit the scattered ends of her composure together, wondering how she could possibly meet Elen at the airport without what the Army testily termed a public display of affection.

But she was barely off the plane when a young man offered a burgundy rose and his arm; he got her luggage, and handed her into a cab, and drove her to a tiny city, parking in front of a Main Street hotel; he collected her bags and led her through a gracious old lobby to an elevator and punched Three.

She hadn't quite known what to expect, but an empty room hadn't been high on her list of possibilities. She tried to pay the cabbie, but he insisted he'd been taken care of. On the dresser, a bottle of Chivas stood flanked by two glasses, another burgundy rose beside it, and a card; she picked it up. "If you're ever in Maine and need a drink, I'll buy." It made her smile, but it was a puzzled, hollow smile: "I am and I do and I'm glad you remembered," she murmured, "but I expected you." She unbuttoned the jacket she had been in for twenty hours and spun the cap from the bottle; she poured three fingers into a glass and raised it, an almost-hurt toast to her aloneness—and in the mirror she met heavy-lidded hazel eyes and a slow, welcoming smile.

"Carpe diem," Elen said softly, pushing away from the bathroom door as Kare turned in startled amazement. "Welcome home, Kare."

She could only watch as Elen came toward her, lean and sinuous as a cat in sharply-creased jeans, a crisply-pressed pale purple shirt *(I bought her that shirt in Austin)*, Corcoran jump boots with those goddamned little silver balls across the toes, a deep red rose in her hand, a deep smile in her eyes. "For you," she said quietly, offering the rose. "My heart."

Kare accepted the lush bloom in both her hands, cradling it gently in her palms. "I'll take better care of it this time," she whispered, knowing she would cry, unable to stop it as Elen took her face between her hands. "Elen—"

"You still wear Chanel." It was a whisper before Elen's lips met hers in gentle greeting. "God, how I've missed you." A soft voice, and a softer kiss; delicately, lips brushed at the dampness tears had left on her face, sharing them before finding her mouth again, kissing her lips one at a time, and then together, a subtle, caressing warmth. "Kare, you have me back."

"I said I'd give anything. Tell me what you want."

"I have it. You're here."

You gave yourself to me, Kare. You trusted me—you risked yourself for me. Words whispered so long ago; she knew what she would have seen in Elen's eyes that first night, had there been light for her to see. "How did I ever doubt that you loved me?"

"Do you know now?"

"I know. God, Elen, I know."

They seemed able only to hold each other. At last Elen's lips brushed her throat and she stepped back; Kare raised a questioning eyebrow. "Just looking," she murmured. "It's the nature of memory—how could I not have remembered how beautiful you are? I saw you in the light."

Softly, Kare laughed. "You always were good at a compliment. Thank you."

"Thank you thank you thank you," Elen smiled.

"Oh, lord. Elen, I can't tell you how it felt to get that telegram. I sat in my office and cried and laughed and cried—I know they think they got rid of me just in time. I must have looked like I'd completely lost it."

"You should have seen me trying to find the Western Union office. They moved it while I was gone. There's a damned hairdresser where it used to be, I tore in yelling, 'where the fuck's the telegram guy? Where'd he go?' I weirded out the old ladies waiting to get their hair blued." Her hands sought her pockets, her smile fading to something small, almost helpless. "When you said you'd been thinking about me—Kare, I was a basket case. I was—" She turned, too late to hide the quick shine of tears. "I'd wanted to call you—I started to a dozen times but I didn't—I didn't know if you—"

"Elen, what's wrong?" Everything—the tension of her, the set of her shoulders, the taut catch of breath—told her how hard Elen was trying to hold onto a hurt too big to be contained for long. "What happened?" Softly, she asked, but Elen only shook her head. Kare reached to touch her shoulder. "Elen, you crashed back into my heart like the wreck of the old number seven," she said quietly. "I couldn't stop thinking about you. Not that I ever stopped, but this was as if—sometimes I almost saw you, like a—a shadow, or—something peripheral, and when I turned you weren't there, but I knew you had been. I'm not religious, or superstitious, but something's feeling very elemental here. Tell me what's going on. Please."

Elen glared at the ceiling. Kare knew the look too well; it was trying-not-to-cry, some tensioning angle keeping tears at bay. "I couldn't call you. Not for this." Her voice was soft and rough. "And I don't want some . . . some psychic space fuck defining us now. I needed you, but when I got your letter all the why went away and all I could see was us being together again—"

"I think you called me whether you ever picked up the phone or not," Kare said quietly. "Please, Elen. Tell me."

Elen drew a breath and hissed it out between her teeth and turned to face her. "Nikki," she said, and Kare's stomach dropped perilously *(still? ogod, still?)* before Elen ran a hand through her hair, and turned as if to sit, but didn't. "She's dead," she said softly.

Kare felt a jolt of something very much like pain. She had wished many things for and from Nikki Cole, but death had never been one of them; when she thought of her—and she had, sometimes—she had only hoped the pain Nikki had been carrying that last day in her office had abated. "Elen, how? When?"

"Last month—August first. She—" She swallowed. "Some sons of bitches they'll never catch killed her for being queer. They beat her to death."

"Oh, Elen, no. My god—"

"She died on a goddamned sidewalk in Cambridge—" Her voice rasped, and then caught; she jammed her hands into her pockets again. "No one here knew her. All they could feel was for how I felt. She was just a name—I couldn't make her exist for them, and it was like—like being caught in that Ionesco play, the one where everybody's named Smith? There was no one to grieve her with, and I— you knew her. She was real to you—I needed the piece of her you had, or—" She sat wearily on the edge of the bed. "Yeah. I never could

get over her without you. I didn't want that to be why I called
you, Kare. She was too much of who we were the last time."

"Oh, god." It was a soft breath of a sigh; Kare sat beside
her on the bed. "Elen, I'm so sorry. It must have been so hard
for you."

Elen shrugged a little. "Yeah. Well."

"So you—" Kare hesitated. "Had you seen her? I
mean—"

"The last time I saw her was Fort Hood. We'd been in
touch, but—" Her shrug was small, pained. "She was in
Provincetown. It's a twelve-hour drive, running legal. I guess
neither one of us—" Hollowly, it hung there. "And I hate that.
I hate that we didn't, because I—oh, shit." She put her elbows
on her knees, and her head in her hands. "Kare, I'm sorry.
Some welcome home."

"You loved her," Kare said gently. "I accepted that a
long time ago, Elen —before I ever left Texas." She reached
to stroke her hand across the short, soft gold of Elen's hair.
"This was—five, six weeks ago? No arrests?"

"Fffft." Elen flipped a hand back over her shoulder,
frustration and derision at once. "Like they give a shit. One
more homo off the streets for all the fucking cops care. If they
caught them they'd give them twenty, reduce it to ten, and
they'd be out in four, ready to pull on their stompin' boots."

Kare got up to retrieve her drink from the dresser. "I had
this—concept of the two of you together," she admitted
quietly. "I had to write to you—I had to try—but I really
thought you'd be with her. And I could have handled that. I
knew she loved you. I couldn't have been sure of anyone else.
I wanted you to be happy, even if it wasn't with me."

Elen stretched her legs out, seeming to study the spit-
shined toes of her boots, before she looked up with a small

smile. "Gracious and generous," she said softly. "That's what my mother said about you. She's still right."

Kare tasted her drink. "How do your parents feel about this? Us?"

"Well, your timing's good. Two months ago you'd have started World War Three." She drew her cigarettes from inside her shirt and lit one. "Dad wasn't dealing with me being gay. Not at all. But when Nikki—that gave him a wake-up call like you read about. He said all he could think when he heard her name on the news was that it could have been me. It didn't hit him when she was 'an unidentified lesbian,' but when she was Nikki—"

"Close to home?"

"Gut shot. So he told me, and I came unglued—" She gave Kare a shaky smile. "I hold everything in for a long time, and then when I cry I cry for everything at once. But you've seen that."

"Yeah," she murmured, remembering the first time she had held Elen while she cried, and how hard it had been then not to offer more than a shoulder.

"So we went fishing for a few days—it was the first time in years we'd done anything together. He and Erin and I used to go, but since she—"

She shaped the fire of her cigarette in the ashtray. "We talked—I don't remember ever talking like that with him. He said it showed him that his approval had nothing to do with my love. That seeing how much her death hurt me made him see it doesn't matter what kind of love it is, it's love and it's real and it matters. And I was feeling—I was scared," she admitted. "Mom accepted me being gay, but he didn't. We got into a real shitstorm one night—he almost hit me. She told him if he ever did, she'd divorce him. It felt like they were coming apart and I was the reason, and I couldn't leave the house because if I did she'd blame him and—Christ, it was a mess. So we did our talking, and then he and Mom took two weeks and went to Aruba. We all needed the time apart." She shook her head with a small laugh. "Not to mention he was a little better equipped to cope with the babbling idiot his kid turned into when I got your letter."

"It couldn't have been that bad," Kare smiled.

"Bad? I was ballistic. Hell, Mom took my car keys away from me." She stubbed out her cigarette. "Then until I heard back I figured you'd probably been drunk and you didn't mean it and you wouldn't wire or write or call or anything and—I chewed my fingernails halfway down to my elbows. Then I didn't believe you were really coming. That's why I didn't go to the airport."

"I go on my knees to you, and this is all the faith you can muster up? I am insulted."

"Oh, and that!" Elen aimed a finger at her; Kare caught it with her own, holding it. "I meant to talk to you about that." She brought Kare's hand to her lips. "Don't you ever go on your knees, Goddess. Not to me or anyone. There isn't anything worth your pride."

"You know where pride goeth, and a little begging goes a long way toward getting a lot of humble. Besides—oh, aren't you bad." Elen had hooked a finger into the waistband of her slacks, a gentle suggestion; Kare took the step needed to put her into the welcome of Elen's arms. "Besides," she murmured as Elen's lips met hers, "you never minded before when I begged you."

Take me. Elen, please take me—do it now, Elen, please now.

Kare felt that shared memory in Elen's kiss, in her hands, in her body; she knew what it had evoked, for she felt it, too: helpless desire, raw and unrestrained, and she remembered how many times she had cried, how many nights she had dreamed, how many small and lonely orgasms she had had, remembering being able to spill those words into the warmth of Elen's being. She shivered, a warm, liquid shiver. "I might yet go on my knees to you."

"Thin fire runs like a thief," Elen murmured against her lips. "You make me so damned helpless."

"That's my line—oh, not fair," Kare whispered, when Elen's lips sought the place below her ear where she put her perfume. "You know that takes the legs right out from under me—"

"How did you know I was ready for you, that night out in the field?" Elen asked, a soft breath of question against her ear; hands slipped softly inside her jacket, smoothing from her waist to her shoulderblades. "How did you know you were the one I wanted?"

"I didn't. I only knew I had to try." Kare rested her forehead against Elen's, helpless in the memory and the feel of them together. "I'd wanted you for so long, Elen. When you offered me that drink—that day was the first time you'd ever called me by my name and god, how you looked when you did it—I was useless all night. You were all I could think about, and every time I looked up you were looking at me and that made me crazy, and when you left it drove me crazy that you weren't there—poor Bill knew something was wrong; he damn near threw me out of the command post. When I saw you out there—" Softly, she laughed. "The indelicate phrase that comes to mind is, 'I creamed my jeans.' You gave me that smile and I just melted."

"Can we talk terrified? All I kept thinking was 'she's a major, you moron, you lay a hand on her and she'll have you cleaning her office floor with a toothbrush until you retire or die.' I don't know if I'd ever have been able to make the first move."

Kare kissed the corner of her mouth. "You made one hell of a second move," she whispered. "I'd never been kissed like that, Elen—and I'd never, ever let anyone be rough with me that way. I'd never wanted to be—possessed, that way. I'm not" —almost shyly, she smiled— "naturally subordinate."

"You knocked my damn socks off when you said take me. Talk about an offer I couldn't refuse." Elen's hands were gentle against Kare's face. "Do you remember the night at the gym a few weeks before we went to the field? Maybe a week after you told me you were gay? I was on curls and you were getting ready for presses and you asked me to spot for you and I dropped the damn bar?" Kare nodded. "I looked over and saw you on the bench and right there—right then—I wanted you. One second you were just my buddy and the next second I was seeing myself pushing up your shirt so I could lick the sweat from between your breasts. And I dropped the bar."

"You dropped the ball, Squirt," she whispered. "I'd have let you lick anything you wanted to."

"God, it made it so hard to work with you. You'd call me into your office and I'd pray for control. I know twice I almost lost it."

"I know exactly when. The same twice I almost did, and one of them—"

"Bucky blew in without knocking—" Kare laughed; Elen was right. "—and I was so close to saying I can't help it, I want you, you make me crazy. God bless his timing. Another two minutes and he'd have caught us cold."

"He'd have caught us hot, Squirt." Gently, she raked her fingers through Elen's hair. "That first night—god, I've thought about that night a lot," she whispered. "My very favorite fantasy. There've been a lot of little o's in the last three years, remembering that big one."

"I've gotten pretty good mileage out of it myself," Elen admitted. "That, and the first night at your house, with the lights on—"

"The car," Kare laughed. "That day out in Lampasas? I didn't think I'd live through it. I hated selling that car."

"You had on that green silk shirt and no bra? Those white shorts? I'm surprised we got as far as Lampasas. I'm surprised we got out of the garage. God, you looked good enough to eat."

"As I recall—"

"Yeah, as I do too," Elen grinned. "Appetizer, entrée and dessert."

"God, I love you," Kare whispered, loving holding her, loving being held by her. "Thank you thank you thank you. It's the first time in so long those memories haven't hurt. I know it was self-inflicted, but—"

"You had help. I knew where you were." Gently, she broke from Kare's embrace. "Kare, I—" She poured a shot of scotch into the second glass, swirled it for a moment, tasted it, took the rest in a swallow. "I might still—Kare, I've never—" She laughed briefly, bitterly. "I took a shot in the dark, but the only time she ever touched me was to slap me upside my face trying to find out about you. I'm still a virgin, or whatever you'd call it. *Ne touche pas*, anyways. It might still be a problem. It's not fair not to tell you."

Kare slipped her arms around Elen's waist, bringing her gently against her; she touched her lips to the back of her neck. "We've got time," she said quietly. "We'll deal with it, honey." She took the glass from Elen's hand. "It's too early for this, Squirt. I've been awake for a day or so, but it's still only ten in the morning to you. And what's this about getting slapped? Take me to her. I'll lay some goddess wrath on the bitch."

"Hardly worth it. I had a sixteen-night stand. She asked me who else I'd slept with. I wouldn't answer. We snarled back and forth a little bit and she belted me. History. And it wasn't that I wouldn't let her touch me; she never tried." She leaned into Kare's warmth, and Kare waited, wondering if Elen would ask; she did, hesitantly. "You?"

"I think one-night stand means one night when you just can't stand it any more—and then can't stand yourself the next morning. One night in Paris. One in Brussels. First names only, and they both looked like you." She huffed a shaky laugh into Elen's hair. "And it isn't that they wouldn't let me touch them; I didn't try." Softly, she kissed the back of Elen's neck. "Will that bother you?"

"Why would it? I wasn't there." She turned in Kare's arms, nuzzling her throat. "I wonder if they know how lucky they were, one night of their lives."

"They weren't what I'd call peak performances. I was dead tired and dead drunk both times."

Elen kissed her, a brief, warm brush of lips, her hand gentle against her cheek. "Speaking of tired, you look beat," she said softly. "If you want to get some sleep, I'll stay with you."

Kare was suddenly crushingly weary; she wished she'd followed impulse and taken the Concorde and to hell with the money. "What day is this?"

"Tuesday the ninth." Elen brought a thick handful of Kare's long coppery hair to her face, loving the softness of it. "Why? You're on leave."

"I need to call Washington before close of business the eleventh. Don't let me forget."

"Are you taking the Pentagon or the command?"

"The offer closes close of business the eleventh. I need to decide by then, but I didn't want to do it without talking to you."

Elen brushed her hair back from her shoulders. "It's your career, Kare."

"It's our life," she said quietly. "I can't plan mine without knowing yours. If I'm going to take my twenty and run, I'll leave the Pentagon for some other waterwalker who wants a make-or-break shot at stars on her shoulder."

"Is that really the prize? A star?"

Gently, Kare disengaged from her embrace. "Provided I don't royally screw up somewhere along the way."

"Like getting caught in a lesbian relationship?"

"That'd do it." She unbuttoned her blouse. "God, I hate to fly. It always makes me feel grubby. I need a shower."

"What about Leavenworth? Didn't you say you'd been offered a Command and General Staff position?" Elen watched in frank appreciation as Kare undressed. Her body was sleek, taut, deeply and gracefully feminine, a lithe, resplendent she-warrior body; she battled back a potent throb of desire. *Let her sleep, you horny bitch. It'd be too fucking male to—*

"Teaching; yes. If I take it—" She shrugged. "I might make full colonel, but the stars will all stay in the sky."

"Isn't that what Bucky used to call the nesting eagle? It lands on your shoulder and shits down your back until you retire?"

"That's Bill. No nesting eagle for him; he got his star this summer."

"Good for him. I really did like him. Did you know he knew about us?"

"I thought he might. But he sent me a dozen roses when I made lieutenant colonel." She stopped at the bathroom door, looking back at Elen. "Speaking of roses, thank you," she said softly. "What was the quote from? I know I should know."

"Faust. That was the bet: 'If ever I say to the passing moment, Linger a while, thou art so fair, then you may cast me into fetters, and I will gladly perish then and there.'" A tiny smile twitched to her as she slipped a hand into a pocket of her jeans. "He sealed it in blood," she said, and opened the blade of a tiny pocketknife.

And the bet was his soul. And she's serious. "Elen, don't. You've bled enough for me," she whispered, and turned from those heavy-lidded hazel eyes before she went naked to her knees to beg.

❏   ❏   ❏

She woke just past midnight to find Elen curled around her back-to-belly in the bed; she smiled, feeling shirt and jeans and bare toes against her own nakedness. "Elliot Ness," she murmured, thinking Elen was asleep, and was surprised by a soft kiss nuzzled into her hair. "Why the pajamas?"

"Because if I was naked too you wouldn't have gotten any sleep, and you needed that worse than you needed my tender kisses all over your body."

"Having clothes on never stopped you from covering my body with tender kisses before," she almost laughed, as Elen's lips rippled down her back and up her arm, ending up nibbling at her earlobe. "Honey, don't. I've got to pee."

Elen let her go; she got in a quick lick with the tooth-brush while she was there, and came out stretching, feeling human again. "God, I'm starving."

"For food, or tender kisses?"

She sat on the edge of the bed, slipping a hand across the thickness of Elen's hair, watching it glint gold in the dim light from the bathroom. "I've eaten in the last two and a half years, but I haven't had you. Can we order tender kisses from room service, or do you have one on you?"

Elen pulled her gently down and gave her one, deep and thoughtful and thorough. "Linger a while," Kare whispered when she could, and felt the smile that twitched to the lips against her own. "Thou art so good at this," she smiled back against the mouth grazing hers, lips and teeth nibbling, tongue lightly teasing; smoothly, Elen took her onto her back. "You'll make me all wet," she warned, her arms going around Elen's neck, holding her there. "Don't start with me, Squirt. You know how I get."

"Squirt." Softly, Elen laughed. "How do you get, Goddess?"

"Demanding, for one—" Kare brought Elen back to her mouth, seeking those talented lips with her own. "God, Elen, I want you—"

"Tell me what you want." Elen went to one knee over her, resisting her kiss, her voice as teasing as the tongue tickling at her ear, circling, probing in, drawing the breath from her before withdrawing to lick wetly against her throat. "Tell me—"

"You know what—oh, god," she almost gasped, when Elen's tongue flickered a warm, suggestive promise around her nipple. "Elen, please—"

Lips traced the line of her jaw, the hollow of her throat, her collarbone; teeth raked gently against the swelling rise of her breast. A thumb rode across her hardening nipple; a warm-palmed hand spread at the small of her back. One denimed knee asked permission to slip between her legs. She granted that, her breath deserting her when that hard-muscled thigh pressed against her. "Tell me," Elen whispered between her breasts. "Tell me, Kare—"

That mouth was at her own again, seeking; she let her teeth risk bruising Elen's lips. She didn't want gentle. Not this time. She had never trusted a lover the way she had trusted this woman one hot October night three years ago; she wanted that again, this second first time. She raked her nails down Elen's shirted back and felt the hard response to her hands, felt Elen's shirt rough against her breasts and the abrasion of denim between her thighs.

"Tell me." It was a ripping breath panted at the corner of Kare's mouth, a scour of lips and cheeks and teeth against each other. "Tell me, Kare—"

"You know what I want—god you know what I—Elen take me! ohmygodyes—" A hand slipped between her legs, a finger probing for her wetness, drawing the need from her in a gasp of words *now, Elen, do it now take me now* before they thrust at the same time, she her hips and Elen deeply into her *god yes! Elen ogod I love you*—and she knew there was no time; there was only wanting her for so long, needing this forever, knowing she was loved as she ascended into that other liquid dimension, an explosive journey there and a weightless wander back to the knowledge of Elen sobbing her name into her throat, her fingers still buried inside her, locked in the depth of her own release; Kare held her, feeling the shudder grip her and finally, slowly, let her go. "Elen—"

"Oh, god," Elen murmured moments later, drowsy against her breast. "Just like a man. One shot and I'm wasted." But when she would have drawn her hand slowly from its wet embrace Kare tightened her thighs, keeping her there. "You did say demanding, didn't you." It was a languid, purring chuckle, her fingers making suggestive exploration. "You warned me not to start."

"I'm warning you now not to stop. Don't stop—" She raised to one elbow, spilling Elen onto her back. "Don't stop," she whispered, and slipped her hand into the neck of a shirt she remembered closed with snaps, not buttons; gently, she split those snaps. "Don't stop—"

"Kare—" Elen's hand stilled against her.

"That's an order." She pressed her lips softly against Elen's throat, kissing her there until the rhythm returned to her hand, and then she nosed the cloth aside, finding the taut rise of her breast with her lips. "Please don't stop, Elen—" She felt the tension in the slender body under hers, and rested her cheek against Elen's breast, letting them both regain the cadence. "This is so good, Elen—oh, god, right there," she breathed, as a long, delicate finger slipped deeply into her, finding the high, slick spot that would rip the control away from her. "Elen—" She had just enough discipline left when Elen moaned *Kare please*—to close her mouth gently over her warm, hard nipple, to feel Elen stiffen against her—

—and Elen buried one hand in her hair, holding her against her breast, gasping *oh—god—Kare* and pulsing into her on each word, and Kare tried not to scream, tried not to bite—and decided, however much longer it was, that what she was doing was regaining consciousness. "Elen?" Arms tightened around her, a shiver coursing through the slim warmth beneath her. "Honey, are you all right?"

"Don't stay away so long next time, hunh?" It was barely a whisper. "We keep this up, they'll have to scrape us off the ceiling."

Her face was still cradled against Elen's breast; softly, Kare let her lips brush her nipple. "I didn't bite you, did I?"

"No."

"I didn't mean to push you, Elen—"

"Yes you did."

"Are you angry?"

"Do I look angry?" She burrowed a kiss into Kare's hair and sighed back against the pillows. "You know what was the best thing about every night after the first night, loving you?"

"Hmmm?"

"Being able to hold you like this. Knowing we'd wake up together."

"God, yes. I hated leaving you that night."

"Six weeks," Elen whispered. "Kare, it's going to go so fast."

Kare put a finger to Elen's lips. "Shhh," she whispered. "Go to sleep."

CHAPTER SEVENTEEN

They had a leisurely breakfast in the cafe of the hotel, Kare delighted by the horseshoe bar, the old photos on the walls, the eggs Benedict; "Why did I have to come to Presque Isle, Maine, to get eggs Benedict this good?" she wondered, and they drank a lot of coffee, recovering from jet lag and loving. They argued over the check, Kare winning with a look Elen recalled from a time when the rank on the collar of the owner of those warning green eyes was all it took to back her down. "Unfair advantage," she muttered, when she realized why Kare had the check in her hand. "Look," she said, on the street in a gloriously bright September day, "don't be grabbing the check like that, Kare—"

"I was prepared to buy two plane tickets to anywhere in the world," Kare said mildly. "I guess I can buy the groceries. I'm fairly certain I have the financial advantage, Elen, so don't argue with me. And I'll get the room, too."

"Like hell you will."

"Don't argue with me about this, Elen."

"Don't pull rank on me, Colonel." It might have stung, but for the tiny grin in the hazel eyes.

"I'm not trying to. I'm saying I expect—and intend—to pay for a trip that was my idea. Unless this burg has a major

181

surprise up its sleeve for me, it looks a hell of a lot cheaper
than six weeks in Paris or Hawaii."

"Is that where you wanted to go?"

"I wanted to be with you. I never expected you to ask
me to come here."

"You said you wanted calm and quiet. This isn't where
we're going; it's just the closest airport to it—hey, where're
you going?"

"Recruiting office." It was across the street; Elen
dodged traffic behind her. "I need to call Washington, remember? Might's well charge Uncle for the call."

"This is only the tenth." Elen caught up with her halfway to the display of antique Navy posters. "I thought we
were going to talk about it."

"We did."

"Well, not a hell of a lot, we didn't. What are you telling
them?"

"Leavenworth." She reached for the door; Elen caught
her wrist.

"Kare, wait! Have you thought about this?" She took
her elbow, steering her away from the door. "Come on.
There's a little park down here; we can talk." When she was
sure Kare would come with her, she gave her back her arm.
"You've been seeing stars ever since I've known you, Kare!
Why give up the chance now? What the hell's going on?"

"Elen, I don't want to spend the next fifteen years
running my ass off— and kissing everybody else's—for a few
pieces of chrome-plated brass. I want a life. I want you in it.
If I go that way I can't have either one."

"But if you don't take it and something happens to us
you've blown your shot! I'm spending the next two years here
anyway, to finish my degree. Take the command tour at
McClellan. It keeps you on the fast track, Kare. Nothing says

you can't flip them a flying bird on your way out the door then, but Christ, leave yourself the door."

"I'm not sure that's the door I want under any circumstances. McClellan would be the last time I'd ever see troops, and they're all that's ever really mattered to me. After that I'd spend the rest of my career in a city I despise, playing politics from dawn to dusk."

"Kare, everything's politics, the minute you step outside your own front door. You know that."

"Of course I know it. I knew Bill Buckman was fighting politics every day of his command tour, but I didn't know he was fighting for his life. Maybe he wasn't. Being a female field-grade officer is like walking a tightrope, Elen. I got on the fast track and the rope got higher and thinner, but at least there was a net. The first thing they'll do when they pin that eagle on my collar is take away the net. One screw-up and they'll hand me a desk in some backwater outpost and wait for me to tell them where to ship my household goods for the last time. Catch me out of the closet and I ship them at my own expense."

She slowed down when they got to the grass of the park. "I've never been a feminist," she said quietly. "You know that; we used to damn near argue over it. I believe in the military and I believe in the basic structure of it. I'd like to see it more equitable for women, and their theory that homosexuals are compromisable is too stupid for words. But within the extant structure, I do believe cream of either sex can rise—as long as you never forget that GI cream isn't the same as civilian cream. Not by any stretch is it the same."

They had walked through a narrow park to stop at the edge of the water; she kicked a rock into the current. "So they've decided I'm cream, but they've based their decision on incomplete data. I'm not up to making sure that data stays

incomplete, and if it's complete, I'm not GI cream." She bent
to pick up a stone, sidearming it halfway across the river.
"You're the missing link in the files, and to keep you missing
I'd have to keep you out of my life. They think I'm in Fort
Worth right now. If I were straight and you were male they
wouldn't mind if you were enlisted or twenty years younger
or—remember Chuckie Cheeseballs? He married an enlisted
woman. Cardinal sin, right? He made captain on the first list.
He beats her. That's common knowledge—and he'll still
make major on the first list. He's arrogant and misogynistic
and not very bright, but they wouldn't mind if I'd married
him. They wouldn't say a word if I came to work every so
often with two black eyes and my arm in a cast, which is how
I saw his wife last. She fell downstairs? Sure she did. But
that'd be okay, because I'd be straight. If I'm lesbian, it'll
affect my work. Due to budget restrictions, the light at the end
of the tunnel has been turned off."

Faintly, Elen smiled. "No, Kare, you never were a
feminist. Not a bit."

"I'm not a feminist. I just understand that arrogant
misogyny is Uncle's idea of a good officer. So I'm arrogant
in refusing men, and misogynist in my official refusal of my
real sexuality. *Voila*: square peg, square hole."

"Try wolf in sheep's clothing."

"Leavenworth's a good post," Kare said quietly. "It's
small and beautiful and drenched in history. Maybe the door
from CGSC opens to a faculty position at West Point, if we
don't work out and I stay in. Or maybe not; I know a guy
who's been there eight years. He was an instructor when I was
there, and he's still there. He loves it. It's calm and quiet and
no one hassles him. He goes in at seven, goes home at four,
and has a lunch hour every day. He meets people from all over
the world. There's a hunt club, for God's sake. It's a country

club post, Elen. I don't need to make any statements for women. I need to survive another two years, and I can do it there. I can't in Washington." She knew Elen was studying her; she watched the river, and finally looked at her. "Tell me what you're thinking. Please, Elen."

"You've really made up your mind?"

"Yes. I have." She searched the hazel eyes; there were no clues there. "Some other woman's going to have to be the first female four-star. I can't pay the price."

"General Dillinger." She said it like tasting it and then offering her a bite, Eve with an apple.

Kare turned from her. "What was the quote? 'If ever I say to the passing moment—' You're it, Elen. I let you go once. I won't—I can't—do it again. Not for eagles and stars—" She could feel her voice tightening in her throat. "Damn it, will you talk to me?"

"I think I'd better quit playing cards for money."

"What?"

"Too lucky in love," Elen whispered. "Too damn Irish lucky in love."

Kare almost reached for her, and caught herself; the park was in view of half of downtown. "Why the hell did you tell me to take it, then?"

"So I can live with myself," she said quietly, "in case you ever regret not doing it because of me. Go call Washington. I want to take you somewhere. It's calm and it's quiet— and it's a long damn ways away from a phone."

CHAPTER EIGHTEEN

"You weren't kidding about the phone, were you," Kare said that afternoon; they were ten miles from the last town or telephone pole, according to the odometer on Elen's glossily-new Chevy pickup. That last pole had been thirty-five increasingly rural miles from the hotel; the roads had gone from fair to bad, and to gravel ten miles ago. Three turnoffs later, grass was growing between little-used tire tracks. For all ten of those miles, there had been nothing around them but deep forest. "How much farther?"

"Ten miles past the moose." Elen braked, smiling at Kare's "omigod!" as an enormous bull emerged from a growing-up old clear-cut to stop in the middle of the road and look at them, the long bell under his chin swaying gently, his immense rack dangling strips of velvet. "Isn't he just classic."

"He's wonderful!" Kare was delighted with him; Elen had said they might see some game, but until now "some game" had been two rabbits and a squirrel, and she'd had no idea a moose might be so huge or so elegantly homely in the flesh. "He's magnificent! How much does he weigh? Can you guess?"

"Three-quarter ton, standing there." She took her foot off the brake and they rolled forward; the moose turned and loped down the road, gangly but still, somehow, graceful.

They followed at a respectful distance for half a mile before
he melted off into the woods. "Well, there. You've seen a
moose."

They saw another one, and two deer and a shy black
bear before Elen turned onto a road Kare wasn't sure she
would rightly call a road before she realized it was a driveway
of sorts, a quarter-mile pair of ruts ending in the yard of a
somnolent log cabin on the edge of a pond; the odometer told
her they were twenty-one miles from the last telephone or
electrical outlet. If war broke out tomorrow, she wouldn't
know and the Army wouldn't be able to tell her, and that was
a glorious thought. "Elen, this is beautiful. This is wonderful!"

"Mom's family built it back in the thirties. I know you
said anywhere I wanted to go, and there's places I'd like to
see, but this is where I wanted to be with you." She keyed a
padlock and pushed open a door leading to one of three rooms,
and gave her a short tour: kitchen, common room, bedroom.
It was rough, rustic: woodstoves and homemade furniture,
fishing rods and rifles on the beams, deer antlers on the walls,
decks of cards and cribbage boards on the windowsills—and
books everywhere, from *The Hunter's Bible* to *Aristotle For
Everybody*. "Don't use the toilet until I see if it works. Dad
said he's been having trouble with the feeder line. There's an
outhouse out back."

"I want to meet them before I go," Kare said quietly.
"Your parents."

Elen looked up from the kitchen cookstove; she had
been rattling back the burner plates over the firebox. "I'm
sorry," she said softly. "I could have taken you to do that
today." Slowly, she crumpled a sheet of newspaper and put
it into the stove; two more followed before she looked up
again. "I thought it might be easier if we had a chance to spend

some time together first. If you—" She looked and sounded almost apologetic. "—got to know me again, before you had to try to get to know them. Was that wrong, Kare? We can go back—"

"No," Kare said gently. She had fallen in love with Elen McNally five or seven times since she had opened a box on an airplane to find a rose and a request; she was doing it again now. "I've never met anyone who thinks of other people the way you do. You really are a sweetheart, you know it?"

You're a sweetheart, Elen . . . I love you even if you are straight. Nikki's voice, from long ago and far away; Kare didn't know what the memory was, but she knew there was one before Elen smiled. "So I've been told," she said, and caught Kare's hand in hers, pulling her close for a kiss that might have been meant as a momentary warmth but turned into something more, something deep and hungry and hard to break away from, but they did, neither of them quite knowing why. "You can scream here," Elen whispered. "Not a soul around for miles."

"Oh, hush. Make your fire."

"My fire's all made," she grinned; Kare pointed her at the stove and went to find the outhouse, two beers on the ride in screaming at her bladder.

❏   ❏   ❏

She had never heard the voice of the loons before; once she had, she knew she would never forget it. "I've never heard anything so beautiful," she said softly; they had been drifting for an hour in the canoe, quiet as the day yawned sleepily behind the ridges and the loons cruised like stately dappled yachts across the sunset reflected in the mirrored pond. There was no breeze to whisper in the trees or lap the water against the rocks; there had only been the occasional call of a chickadee in the silence, and when the loon finally raised his ghostly voice it fit so well it didn't occur to Kare to be uneasy in the eerie cry. She had been watching him, saw him open his beak, knew it was him to make that ethereal sound. Across the water, his mate spoke softly back to him. "I've never heard such quiet. I don't know how you stood to be away from here so long, Elen."

"I didn't, very well. The Army's so noisy." Her smile was tiny, reminiscent. "I didn't lie to Bucky when I said I was homesick the day your orders came. I was halfway to DFW when I knew I had to talk to you instead of going AWOL." She rested the paddle across her thighs. "I always took my leave for Christmas. This is another world again in the winter." She looked across the pond, and made a sound with her voice, a hollow, almost cooing sound; both loons looked toward them, and cooed back at her. "No loons in winter." Kare had never realized what a deeply susurrous voice Elen had, what a gentle voice; listening to her, here in this silent world, was like listening to poetry.

> "The pond misses them, I think,
> in the winter. The ice talks—
> when it freezes, you can hear it
> sing, and echo off the ridges.
> The snow talks: different kinds of snow
> have different voices.
> But the loons are gone in winter, and
> even if they could stay,
> Artemis commands them to silence."

She stopped, deferring to the voice of the loon, and Kare felt this world lonely in their absence. "But the weasels turn into ermines, and—look." She reached to touch Kare's knee, pointing with her other hand to the sky. "There he is, Kare. There's your eagle."

He came in low over the pond, white head and tail brilliant against the dark ridge, six feet of wing quivering in currents they couldn't feel; the loons cried out in strident alarm as he skimmed over the water. There was a great splash and then he lifted, wingtips skimming the water for two strokes, a fish squirming in his talons as he pulsed toward the ridge; the women could hear the powerful throb of flight. Shaken by the cruel beauty of him, by the way he had split the silence of the evening with his violence, until he had flown over the ridge Kare watched him, hearing the loons cry after him in distress. "Why are they afraid of him?" she finally asked. She knew without asking that they were.

"He eats their eggs." Elen had been smoking; up here, she rolled her own. She dropped the butt into the water, and tiny fish snapped at it. "He's beautiful and majestic, but he's a cruel bastard, and a lazy one. You'll not see him hunt that way very often; not for fish. He lets the osprey hunt, and then takes it away from her. Sometimes he hurts her." The surface of the pond still shimmered in his wake; he was gone, but his disturbance lingered. "You can see he's good enough at fishing. He'd just rather dominate."

Elen wouldn't let her help with dinner that night, lobster and artichokes; Kare sat watching the easy skill of her lover at the old cast-iron cookstove, four roses in a canning jar on the table (she knew which one was Elen's heart), a soft and lovely barred feather in her hands: an osprey feather, Elen said when she asked, picked from the water one day after the eagle had robbed that mother of her catch. At the base of the feather was a rusty stain.

And late that night, way after supper, way after Elen had made long, slow love to her, way after sleepy talking, she woke to the urgent cry of the loons, that vibrant, ululating call of distress; she listened, and Elen woke enough to hold her when she cried.

❑   ❑   ❑

There was a doe with twin fawns across the pond in the morning, and they watched them with their coffee, Kare quiet and Elen respectful of it until she brought her a third cup; then she asked gently. "What happened last night?"

"Something upset the loons." She watched a large bird soaring looping circles high over the water. "Is that the eagle?"

Elen glanced up. "Osprey."

Sometimes he hurts her.

"You can tell by the wings. The eagle's got a straight leading edge. The osprey has elbows." She whistled a high, piercing note, and got one back, and a comfortable hoo from one of the loons; the osprey didn't bother them. "Something upset the goddess, too," she said quietly. "Can you tell me?"

The coffee was strong, black, bracingly good; she could smell the stove, that sharp woodsmoke scent. One of the loons raised up on the water for a flap of wings before settling back down to preen. Overhead, the osprey keened her shrill whistle; somewhere in the woods, a squirrel chuttered, and a chickadee sang. "I don't want it to end," Kare said softly, and got up before she started to cry again. She went down to the dock and slipped out of her clothes and dove, and swam halfway across the pond and back while Elen sat on the porch, chilled by wondering if Kare already regretted her Leavenworth decision.

"It was the eagle," she said, dripping on the dock; Elen had brought her a towel but she just held it, not using it. "You didn't say there's an eagle. You said there's my eagle. And I felt this—this idiotic swell of blind patriotic pride, and the loons started up and he caught the fish and you said he was a cruel lazy bastard taking what isn't his and I thought of half the bird colonels I've ever known and god, I don't want to be one!" The tears came; she fought to control her voice. "I don't even want to go back. I will because I'm not pissing away eighteen years and walking without my retirement, but I don't want their damned eagle. And I know if they give it to me I'll take it. And I know they'll give it to me about six months before I could retire. They think if they do they'll have me for another three or four years, and then they can dangle West Point and a little tin star in front of me like carrots and like a good little donkey I'll chase them and they'll have me for another five or six. That's what they think. It's no less fucking just because it's my mind they're doing it to, and when I allow it and take money for it, it makes me a whore. God, I've been their whore for eighteen years."

Elen took the towel from her hands and draped it around Kare's shoulders; she was shivering. "No," she said gently. "You loved it, Kare. Whores don't do it for love."

"But I don't love it anymore! Maybe I did for the first fifteen, but what does it make me for the last three and the next two? I'm only going back for the money—"

"So you go back to a job you don't like for a period of time you think you can endure? If that makes you a whore this country's full of them. Take their eagle, Kare. The osprey wins one when you do. You grab that bird by the balls and put the ol' BB Cole squeeze to it, and fuck 'em back by walking at twenty with a fat fish they'll have to give you once a month for the rest of your life. That isn't being a whore, Kare. That's beating them at their own game."

❏   ❏   ❏

"Who's this, Elen?" Kare called the next afternoon when a pickup truck with ten-day plates pulled into the driveway; Elen was in the little bathroom, trying to figure out why the toilet wouldn't fill from the gravity-feed water system. She came out wiping her hands and squinted through the kitchen window.

"Well, I'll be damned. He just couldn't stand me having a new truck; he had to get one too. That's Mom and Dad."

"Oh," Kare said, small-voiced; she hadn't expected them until Sunday. She had planned to be bathed and in clean clothes, not braless in a ragged old T-shirt and cutoff fatigue pants with her hair wrapped in a bandanna, looking as if she'd spent the last hour cleaning the woodstove, which she had; she and the kitchen were a mess. "Oh, boy."

"Ay, dos gringos! Como frijoles?" Elen greeted them from the door, stepping out. "You're early! We're not ready for you, eh? We smell bad."

"Thanks for pointing that out to them," Kare grumbled under her breath, a glance in the mirror over the sink confirming that she looked like Cinderella ante-godmother; she got rid of the bandanna, at least. "God, let them like me," she whispered, and went out to face inspection.

Liz McNally met her halfway up the steps with a smile so genuine Kare had to return it; she wrapped Kare into a warm mother's hug. "You're absolutely beautiful," Liz whispered in her ear, and gave her a kiss on the cheek, soot and all. "Welcome to our family, Colonel Dillinger; I had to call you that once! Now can I call you Kare?"

"God, I should hope so," Kare laughed, surprised into it by the unexpected warmth. "You take first meetings to an art form, Mrs. McNally. Thank you."

"Oh, please not Mrs.! Liz or Mom or whatever you're comfortable with, dear, but not Mrs. unless some obscure

military regulation demands it, which I doubt." She kept
Kare's hand, squeezing gently. "Ezra, stop showing off your
new toy and come see this gorgeous child Elen's brought us."

This one won't be as easy. It was all Kare could think
as she brought her hand up to meet the one Elen's father
offered. "I'm glad to finally meet you, sir. Elen speaks highly
of you."

"I'll paddle her for lying." His grip was warm and firm,
his dark brown eyes there to search her own, searching his;
each of them knew the other was scared half to death. "And
don't call me sir, Colonel. I wasn't an officer and I'm still not
a gentleman. Ezra's just fine."

*But not Dad. Oh well; at least he smiled when he said
it.* "Ezra, then. And I'm Kare."

"I was in Germany for a while, in '43, '45. 'Course the
circumstances were a little different."

"I guess they probably were. Who were you with?"

"Hundred'n-first."

"Bastogne?"

He coughed, and swallowed; she knew the battle-worn
soldier's reluctance to tell the old hard tales. "Ayuh."

"A small and elite club you belong to."

"It gets smaller all the time. Not many of us left."

"I sure wish sometime you'd tell me what MacAuliffe
really said."

He grinned and so did she, and they all breathed tiny
sighs of relief and went to admire the new truck and unload
the supplies. Ezra and Elen tackled the water, and Liz helped
Kare finish the stove and clean up the outrageous mess she
had made, and by the time cards were dealt for Oh Hell after
supper Kare was calling Liz Mother Mac and was confident
enough of Ezra to trump an ace he led to her void suit. "That's
war, Colonel," he threatened, and she scooped in the trick and

led the ace of trump, setting him soundly. "Spoils to the victor, Ez, and all you won is the deal."

It was strange that night, sleeping in the same room, Liz and Ezra in one bed, she and Elen in the other, but Elen, seemingly unconcerned by the presence of her parents, wrapped arms and legs around her and kissed the back of her neck and went to sleep. Kare and Ezra listened to each other breathe for a long time before Kare finally thought, oh, to hell with this, and subsided into the safety of Elen's warmth, but five hours later she almost came out of her skin when a male hand on her T-shirted shoulder shook her awake and a gruff voice said, "The fish're bitin', Colonel. You want to hear what MacAuliffe really said, unass that bed and get your coffee. The boat leaves in ten minutes."

She yawned and drank coffee while he paddled them to a secret spot on the pond, barely awake enough to worry about the fly line swirling around her head so close she could hear it near her ears but never touching her, and he fished with silent intensity until the sun came up, then sat to open his pocketknife and slit the pale belly of a fine trout. "Balls," he said.

"I figured."

"No, that's for this being a female." He showed it to her, filled with roe. "That's just what they say he said," he grinned, and told her what the general had really uttered when he was ordered to surrender, and back in the cabin, Elen and her mother heard Kare's laugh ring across the water.

Elen watched through binoculars as her father taught her lover how to fly fish; she didn't know when Ezra had ever let anyone but his second daughter wield that delicate bamboo rod. "Keep your wrist straight," she murmured from the shore, the glasses trained on the canoe, and something struck the fly and she grinned in helpless pride as Kare struck back and played the fish to the net, beginner's-lucking it from strike to catch. She took a picture when they came back, Kare and Ezra with their arms buddied around each other and grins on their faces and a two-pound trout held between them; as much as Bill Buckman treasured his photograph of Elen and Kare, Elen would treasure the one of Kare and her father. They had trout for breakfast, so fresh it curled in the skillet, and while Elen and Liz did the dishes, Kare and Ezra went for a walk.

"They seem to be getting along," Liz said.

"Do you like her, Mom?"

Liz turned to her daughter. "All I have to do is look at her look at you," she whispered, tears in her eyes. "She loves you, Elen; my god, she loves you with everything in her. How can I not like her?"

❏   ❏   ❏

"Investment consultant," Ezra said, when Kare asked what he had done before he had retired. "Soon's I had enough money to be able to do it as a hobby, I quit. Now I only risk my own—and a few other familial screwballs who trust me with their financial lives."

Kare thought of eighteen years of savings, a handsome sum in CDs and an IRA. "Want another client?"

"What are we talking?" he said, and she told him, and he looked at her with one eyebrow raised when she was finished. "Not bad, Colonel."

She shrugged. "I've got a fairly good salary and almost no expenses. If the market's good I buy houses; if it's not I live in the bachelor officers' quarters. Kids and cars eat it up, and I don't have kids and I buy used cars."

"Keep that IRA, but if you've got CDs coming mature don't just roll them over. I've got a hunch interest rates are going through the roof here shortly. Let me play with it for a while, and then when those rates happen I'll get you locked into some real interest." And he waved a hand when she said commission. "Nah. When you make enough, I'll steal some. More fun that way."

They walked. She noticed with a small smile that they were in step, and had been for half a mile; she could have called cadence. A horsefly buzzed around her head; she swatted at it four times before she knocked it down and stepped on it, and within ten paces they had adjusted their steps back to unison. "Can I ask you something?" she said finally, but when he had glanced at her in question she didn't quite know how to proceed. "Elen's mentioned that she had a sister, but we never seem to get around to talking about her—Erin?"

He sighed. "Erin died when Elen was thirteen. It doesn't much surprise me that she doesn't talk about her. It's not something any of us are good at."

"Can I ask what happened?"

"She was fifteen," he said quietly. "She—" Helplessly, he shrugged. "She was healthy and strong—played sports, all of that—she had a heart attack. She just died in her sleep. They couldn't really give us a reason. She just died."

"My god, that must have been hard," Kare said softly. "I'm sorry, Ezra. I shouldn't have brought it up."

He huffed out a resigned breath. "Yeah. It was hard. But I don't mind talking if there's more you want to know. It's easier with—" strangers, he almost said, and bit it back, and knew by her brief, pained smile that Kare knew what he would have said.

"How did Elen take it?"

He shoved his hands into his pockets, slowing his pace, watching the road in front of his feet. "How did Elen take it," he murmured, and Kare knew she had struck a deep, raw nerve; she wished she'd kept her mouth shut. "You got anything you look back at in your life and know in your heart you were so wrong you'd sell your soul to go back and change it?"

"Leaving Elen," she said quietly, daring the truth.

He glanced at her, his eyes saying she might never know what that mistake had meant to Elen. "By the time you did that, she was damnwell used to love walking out on her." His voice wasn't cold and she knew he hadn't meant to hurt her, but he had; he saw that and reached to squeeze her fingers. "I'm sorry. It may be the truth, but you didn't deserve it that way."

"It's okay," she murmured, returning the hug his hand was giving hers, and they let each other go.

"I said it because Liz and I lost one child," he said slowly, "and seemed to forget we had one left. We didn't take care of her. We were so busy trying to get through it ourselves we didn't look at her to know—" He stopped, and shook his head, looking at the sky; Kare averted her eyes, knowing he'd hate her if she saw him cry. "What does a thirteen-year-old know about death? How could we think she was dealing with it when we couldn't? God, she must have needed us and we weren't there for her—"

He stepped out again so suddenly it took Kare a few steps to catch up with him. "Then I lost my dad and mother in an accident just a year after Erin—I looked at it that way. I lost them. Elen lost her Gram and Grampa, too, and we blew it again. Liz took care of me and no one took care of Elen. At least when Erin died she had my folks. She got real close to them, and then they—you see how she looks now? Hard as a rock and thin as a rake? When she graduated high school she weighed two hundred pounds. That's what we did to her. We finally got her into therapy, but that's a goddamned poor substitute for five years of shitty parenting. We abandoned her."

"Ezra, give yourself some slack. You did your best—"

"My best was piss-poor." His voice sounded like a rockslide in a gravel pit. "And then I acted like a complete and utter jerk when she told us she was gay. I worried about me. I worried about what my friends would think if they found out. I worried about what the neighbors would say. I failed her again. When I held her while she cried for Nikki, it was the first time I'd ever given her anything she really needed."

"I'd say you're on a roll," she said quietly; he looked a wary question at her. "I knew I had two strikes against me coming in. I'd already broken her heart once, and I'm seventeen years older than she is. I didn't expect you to trust me or accept me, no matter how much Elen told me not to worry. I almost threw up when you pulled into the yard yesterday. I was that scared."

"No more than I was," he said gently. "I had no intention of liking you, lady, but I do, and I don't mean to bruise you again, but I understand selfishness and regret. You looked at your life, not hers, and it's nothing I haven't done to her. We're both damned lucky she's giving us another chance, and you look like a hell of a good risk to me. And I don't think you're too old for her. Look at those eyes, for god's sake. She's older than I am, sometimes. You're old enough, not too old."

Kare couldn't help the tears; she swiped at them. "I'm sorry," she said shakily. "I always cry when I fall in love."

It startled him, a warm, bashful surprise; he put an arm around her for a rough, brief hug. "It's not too hard to love someone who loves your kid, Kare. Jesus, I can see how much you do."

❏   ❏   ❏

They stayed for lunch, and even though Kare and Elen protested: "You just got here," from Elen, and "You said you'd teach me to roll-cast," from Kare, they left anyway with a promise to be back in three or four days with ice and beer and groceries. "They're great," Kare said. "God, your dad— he blew me away, Elen. He really did. What a sweetheart."

"It's a recent phenomenon. I wish it hadn't taken Nikki dying to get him there, but—" She shrugged, a small, sad shrug. "It kind of makes me feel like she didn't die in vain. Softens the edges of a real sharp 'why' for me." And she looked up with a smile. "So. Pretty good in-laws?"

"I can't begin to tell you," Kare murmured, and it was late that afternoon, when they were tired from a swim, lying naked on the dock, listening to their loons talk to loons on the lake a half-mile upriver, when Elen said quietly, "You never talk about your parents, Kare. Are they still alive?"

"Yes."

"Is it not a good relationship?"

"There's no relationship. We haven't spoken for twenty years."

"Damn. I'm sorry, Kare."

They were quiet for a while, fingertips touching. The loons yodeled.

"They legally disowned me when they found out I was gay."

"Jesus, Kare. That's incredibly cruel."

"They're ruthless and shallow. A lot of very rich people are, I think."

The loons finished their conversation, and there was nothing but the sound of a light late-afternoon breeze in the woods; shortly even that would fade and the silence would settle upon them. Kare sought Elen's fingers with her own, wrapping around them, and she listened to the trees for a long while before she said softly, "I was in Washington in '75. A friend of mine had tickets to the symphony at Kennedy Center. I saw them. They saw me. Jay had his arm around me. I was in evening dress, hair up, heels, war paint, the whole nine yards. I couldn't have looked any straighter—and they turned their backs on me."

Elen's fingers flexed hard against hers. "You're sure they knew you?"

"Yeah." She sat up; Elen did, too, and rolled and lit a cigarette. "Jay was blown away. He said, 'those people just turned their backs on you, who in the hell are they?' And I said, 'they're my parents.' He took me home and let me cry on his shoulder—" Shakily, she smiled. "Imagine my surprise when I woke up naked with him. My one and only night with a man. But he was sweet."

She picked Elen's cigarette from her fingers and took a taste. "So your folks are a bit of a treasure to me," she said quietly. "They only had to be civil, and they were loving."

Softly, across the pond, the loons hooed. They looked across the water to see the graceful dark birds drift by one another, yards apart but still in contact. "Do they mate for life?" Kare asked softly.

Elen glanced at her. "Yeah," she said quietly. "Yeah. They do."

CHAPTER NINETEEN

She was amazed by the things Elen could talk about; they had a long and complex conversation about the psychology of military strategy, and Kare knew she had worked with field-grade officers, majors and colonels and generals, who didn't understand as much as this twenty-four-year-old three-year veteran whose only strategic training had been two years in an operations shop under a captain who was sharp but not brilliant. "Where do you get this stuff, Elen?"

Elen shrugged. "I read Sun Tzu and Homer. You told me to, remember?" A smile Kare didn't understand twitched to her. "I've got good retention. I'm told the road to hell is paved with it."

It amazed her, too, how comfortable they were with silence between them. Strategy took up fixing dinner, and eating it, and doing the dishes, but when they wound down and nothing came to fill the space they weren't uneasy with having, for the moment, nothing to say. Kare read: *The Art of War*; there was a copy on a bookshelf in a corner, and that amazed her; Elen worked *The New York Times* Sunday crossword in ink, murmuring clues to herself. It occurred to Kare that what they were doing was learning to live together again, and she spent long enough captured by the warmth that gave her, not turning pages, that Elen asked quietly, "What has Master Sun said to catch you so firmly?"

"Nothing." Her smile was almost shy. "Nothing. I was just loving you."

That smile: god, those eyes. Kare thought she would dissolve. "I never stopped loving you," Elen said softly. "I tried to tell myself I didn't still love you, but I always knew I was lying."

Kare closed her book.

Elen capped her pen.

But when her need was strong and her hand slipped down the tautness of Elen's belly, searching, drawn to that smooth warmth even as Elen was finding her own, when her fingers brushed the soft hair at the tops of her thighs Elen's hand touched her wrist, a silent refusal.

"Oh, god—" She drove her face into Elen's throat, desire and frustration wrenching the near-moan from her. "Elen, please! Please let me touch you. Don't do this to us—"

"Don't blame me! God damn it—" She was out of the bed too quickly for Kare to catch her, bouncing off the partly-open door, cursing for that pain, or the other. "Kare, I can't! I freeze! I'm sorry! Do you think I enjoy this? Do you think I don't want you? Jesus, don't blame me for this—" Her voice broke, a ragged cry deteriorating into a whisper. "I've tried. Every time we make love I try to let go and it won't—I can't—" She turned, a shadow in skin and moonlight. "I'm sorry, Kare."

"Elen, no!" She was quick, too; she caught her at the kitchen door, grabbing her arm because there was nothing else to grab. "Christ, you're buck naked, where do you think you're going? The mosquitos'll eat you alive!" Elen tried to twist away from her, reaching for the door; Kare held on. "Elen, don't fight me. Honey, don't—" Taller, stronger, she captured Elen against her, pinning her arms, holding her, and Elen collapsed; she cried, deep, rasping sobs that hurt them both, and Kare tried to keep her on her feet and couldn't. She prayed briefly for her back and gathered her into her arms, taking her back to the bedroom, giving her gently to the bed they shared, and she slipped in beside her and took her close against her. "It's okay," she whispered, knowing it wasn't. "Elen, it's all right, honey. I love you. Shhh—"

Elen's words came back to her: *I keep everything inside, and then when I cry, I cry for everything at once.* This was more everything than Kare was sure she could handle. Elen was huddled tight around herself, not just crying; she was crying something, shivering in her arms. Kare listened, and finally, a word at a time, she made it out. "I'm sorry, god, don't leave me, don't go, I'm sorry, don't leave me—"

God, she must have needed us and we weren't there for her—

Erin. Did she ever cry for her? "Elen, no. Don't apologize—baby, I won't leave you. I'm here, Squirt. I'm here, I won't—"

Don't tell her you won't leave her. In five weeks you'll be in Kansas.

"I'll come back," she whispered. "Elen, I'll always come back to you."

But planes fell out of the sky, and drunks crossed the center line, and hearts that still loved stopped beating, and she could say always and wish it were so, but there were no guarantees; you could say always, but you couldn't always beat the odds. "Elen, I love you." She had never felt so inadequate, having only that to say.

"Don't leave me—"

"I love you. I'm with you, honey. I love you." And remembering Nikki, haunted by Erin, she whispered, "Carpe diem, Elen. All we ever have is now."

❑   ❑   ❑

She woke to a sound she only barely recognized, and sat up to find the sun high and Elen's side of the bed empty and she listened, finally identifying the thwack of ax against wood. "Oh, lord," she murmured, and got up and found yesterday's clothes and tugged them on, and she staggered to the kitchen, finding the stove built and the coffee made and her favorite mug on the counter with a slip of paper rolled inside it; she pulled it out: "I'll love you as long as there's a diem to carpe about. I'm okay. Have your coffee and come talk to me. Thank you thank you thank you."

She went to pee, and came back for a coldwater wash and poured her coffee and went to the splitting side of the woodshed. "Hey, there."

"Hey, yourself." Elen steadied a chunk of maple on the chopping block and brought the heavy-headed ax down onto it; it halved neatly.

"Did you sleep?"

"Yeah." She let the ax fall to the block, just enough force and weight to make it stick. "Pretty well, actually." She glanced up, and away again, shyly. "I guess I kind of lost it for a minute. Thank you for staying with me."

"How could I have left you?"

Elen shrugged a little, and nudged at a stick of wood with her toe. "You could have let me go, I guess."

"So I could find your bloodless corpse in the morning, sucked dry by the mosquitos? I don't think so, Squirt." She sipped her coffee, leaning against a massive hemlock. "Elen, we need to talk about this," she said softly. "Are you ready to do that?"

"Look, you just got up—"

"I'm awake. If you don't want to talk about it yet, say so, but admit it."

"You won't leave it alone, will you."

"No. It's too important, Elen. It hurts you too much." Elen sat on the chopping block with a huge and shaky sigh. "So we talk."

"I love you with all my heart, Squirt, but I'm not about to talk sex to a hot-tempered woman with an ax in her hand. Come sit on the porch."

She offered a hand; Elen looked at her for a long moment before she took it, and allowed Kare to pull her to her feet, and accepted the warmth of the hug Kare offered. "Kare, I'm sorry," she whispered. "God, I hate this."

"Stop apologizing. This isn't your fault. If it was you'd have found it and fixed it by now. Come—" She snugged an arm around Elen's waist, taking her through the kitchen, pouring coffee for them both, and on the porch she let Elen make a cigarette and stole it, and waited while she rolled again for herself. "Elen, what do you feel when that happens?"

"Right to it, huh." Elen looked out across the pond. There were no deer, no moose, no ospreys or eagles or loons; there were no excuses. "I just freeze up," she said at last. "I lose—the desire. I lose the—warmth. I just feel cold. Physically cold. I still love you, and need you, but I lose the want."

"What do you think, when it happens? What goes through your mind?"

Most of Kare's cigarette burned down while she waited; she could see Elen trying to go back, trying to remember; she could see the hurt. *God love her; she's a hell of a lot more tired of this than I am.*

"I don't know." Elen looked drawn and tired; her words sounded that way, too. "I don't think I think anything. I mean—I know I'm hurting you, and I hate that. I probably think, not again. Because I do try, Kare. I do."

"I know you do." She knew that last night—and all the times before—when her hand got somewhere below Elen's ribs she felt her tensing up, and still she tried—and Elen let her. Elen tried, too.

"But to say there's any word-thoughts—no. I just feel cold, and—empty. Like—like a cleaned fish. No guts and a big hole in my belly."

Kare smiled sickly, remembering Ezra showing her the roe-filled inside of a trout as if ten minutes ago that being hadn't been alive and burstingly ready to give life, before his thumb scooped out those guts and dropped them into the water, where the trout's own kind argued over them.

"And—" She sniffed a quick breath that sounded like she was warning tears she wasn't in the mood for them. "I flashback," she said, her voice soft and rough and hurt. "To him. To when I lost control of that. Thinking I could handle something and finding out I couldn't. He really hurt me—" That sharp breath came again; the tears were closer this time. "It was no options. Have you ever been powerless? It feels like I've spent my life that way. Things happen and I don't have any control. I can only . . . take the rape."

"Do you remember last night, what you said after we went back to bed?"

"No."

"You kept saying you were sorry," Kare said quietly. "And asking me not to leave you. As if the two were connected."

"Well, how much of this shit are you supposed to put up with? Jesus—"

"If I ever leave you, Elen, this won't be why. It isn't between us, it's just with us." She leaned forward to take one of Elen's hands in both of hers. "The first night, honey. At the hotel? I pushed a little and it worked for you. Why then?" "I don't know." She withdrew her hand from Kare's. "I'll cry," she whispered. "If you touch me I'll just cry and we won't get anywhere." She drew a shaky breath. "Maybe you should just force the issue."

"I can't do that, Elen. You're afraid of something, and forcing you can only make it worse." She sat back, looking across the water; a moose had come out on the far shore, but she didn't mention it. "Elen—" She was afraid of this question, afraid of being wrong. "How did you feel when Erin died?"

Elen closed her eyes. She drew on her cigarette, but it was dead between her fingers; she relit it before she found her voice. "About the same," she whispered. "Like God just stuck his omnipotent dick up my ass."

Kare wished they were in bed. She wished they were naked, skin to skin, so she could curl herself around this hurt and try to take some of it into herself, to help absorb it.

"We were so close," Elen said softly. "Best friends. They said she died around two in the morning, and I—" She got up, paced to the end of the porch, stood there; Kare ached to go to her, and knew she couldn't. "I didn't know. I just slept. Right across the room from her and I didn't" —she hissed a breath between her teeth; Kare had heard that same breath drawn by people in deep physical pain who were trying not to scream— "do anything," Elen whispered. "I didn't do anything. All she did was stop breathing, and if I'd heard that—"

"Elen, that wasn't your fault! My god—"

"I know! Jesus, Kare, haven't you ever had anything your head knew and your heart refused? I can know and be told but it doesn't change the fact that if I'd been awake or if I'd waked up I could have at least tried and not just slept through my sister dying eight feet away from me! I wasn't and I didn't and she died. Fate fuck. Cosmic rape. Like Nikki said, life sucks and then you die. Oh, Kare—"

Wearily, she sat, running both hands through her hair, holding her head for a long, silent moment; at last she looked up. "I know what you're trying to say," she said quietly. "You think I'm afraid to accept your love, that if I do—because I'm afraid of losing you. Kare, I know you love me."

"Elen, you just said it," she said softly. "Haven't you ever had anything your head knew and your heart refused? You know, but you're afraid to take me inside you, and by refusing that physically, you refuse me emotionally. You told me once it was the men, and I'm sure they're part of it, especially Hogle, but I think the promiscuity was a physical manifestation of an emotional cry: you were hoping someone could penetrate the barrier you'd put up to shield yourself from getting hurt again, and all you got was hurt again. It's like the tar baby. You get stucker and stucker."

"Tar baby's racist," Elen said hollowly. "Can't use that one anymore."

"I'm fighting for my life; I'll use whatever I have to. Elen, I can't promise you I won't die. I can't promise we'll always love each other; there is no always. I can promise I'll love you as long as I'm able. And I can surely promise you that the only love you'll ever get in life is what you take when it's in front of you. Carpe diem, Elen. That's all there ever is."

The silence was long, Elen's breathing tight and shallow; she wasn't crying, Kare thought, so much as the hurt she didn't have room enough to hold was leaking out her eyes. When at last Elen spoke, her voice was very soft. "I need to be alone for a while."

"That's all right, honey. Would you like me to drive into town, or—"

"I need you to be here," she whispered. "I'll just go around the pond." She stood, starting away; she stopped, and turned back. "What about you? I take off and leave you; are you okay?"

"I'm okay. Go ahead."

Elen came to her, taking her gently from her chair, and steered her to the edge of the porch to stand behind her; she aimed a finger at the ridge across the water so Kare could sight down it. "The tallest tree. Erin's there, and Nana, and Gram and Grandad. That's where I'll be." She buried a kiss into Kare's hair. "First rule of the woods: never go into them without telling someone else where. I do love you, Kare. Believe it."

❏   ❏   ❏

Kare read. She walked up to the road, and found a thicket of late raspberries; she picked enough into her shirt for a pie, and went back to find a recipe written in an old and spidery hand, and talked the woodstove into baking it up for her without burning it.

She finished the crossword Elen had started last night.

She borrowed Elen's fly rod to practice Ezra's teachings; off the end of the dock she caught a huge, ugly fish. She looked at it when she had the hook out of its lip, and thought about killing it and cleaning it, and gave it back to the water; she put the rod back in the canoe. She wondered why it had been easier to kill a sleek and beautiful trout than to think of killing an ugly grey fish with a mouth that made her think of leeches.

She swam. She sat naked and dripping, drying, on the end of the dock, and watched the tallest tree on the ridge across the pond.

She went to the cabin for soap and shampoo, and swam again with her bath.

At four she made a drink, chipping ice off the dwindling block in the ice box. She dug into the tinderbox by the cookstove and came up with a months-old *Maine Sunday Telegram*, and read every word but the classifieds. She did the Jumbles, the cryptoquip, both crosswords.

She made another drink. "Come home, Elen."

There was a handsome brass bell mounted outside the kitchen door. "If you ever need me, ring hell out of it," Elen had said their first day. "I can hear it for miles." She leaned in the kitchen door, looking at the bell every now and again. Once, she reached, but she only touched the thong on the clapper.

She browsed through the icebox, finding ground beef that smelled as if it ought to be used. She made spaghetti sauce.

She poured a third drink. She watched the sky think about the beginnings of sunset, and tapped the brass bell with a long fingernail. "Elen, come on."

She found two flashlights with batteries. She thought about coyotes and bears; she worked the action and checked the bore of an old Winchester thirty-thirty hanging on the wall, and found bullets in a cabinet on the living room wall. She studied the map hanging on the wall.

She almost knocked Elen down the steps when she headed out the door.

"Whoa! Night hunting's illegal, Goddess. Where you off to?"

"Out to find you, you simple shit. It's about twenty minutes away from darker than Dick's hatband out there."

"And you're going out flailing around in it not knowing shit from shinola? Honey, I know when dark is. I'll always be home by it."

"And I'm better in it than you think I am."

Elen smiled, a those-eyes smile. "I live in hope of finding that out."

"You shithead," Kare whispered, and they held each other for a long, needing moment before they kissed each other gently. "Are you okay?"

"Okay and starved. I smell s'ghetti. Make cook, woman."

"You kiss my ass."

"I'll kiss anything you let me, your lovely ass being about third from the top of my wish list." She kissed Kare's throat instead, but her hands roamed to caress the threatened part; Kare broke smiling away from her.

"Set the table, hungry kid, or we'll never eat tonight." She cooked the pasta, and made a salad, and spent a few minutes picking raspberry twigs out of Elen's hair. "Where the hell have you been? You're a mess."

"I took a header down the ridge. No biggie. What'd you do all day?"

"Frigged around. Made a pie. Took a bath."

"I need one too. I worked up a sweat." And after they ate she went down to the dock and splashed into the pond, the occasional bat whirring softly past her head while she had her swim.

They sat on the porch, braving the mosquitos, and had a drink, Kare in the old cane rocker she liked, Elen in front of her on the porch floor; they listened to the night. "What did you learn across the pond?" she asked quietly, remembering asking a similar question one day four years ago, the day she had looked into those heavy-lidded eyes to know with a slow, warm jolt that she would love this woman, and she knew by Elen's sidelong consideration that she remembered that day, too.

"That gaining someone I can dare to love is worth how hard it might be to give up something I've been for too long," she said softly. "Kare, I feel like there's only ever been two places in my life: without you, and with you." She tasted her scotch and looked out at the darkened pond. "Without you feels like the motor pool in July. Work and sweat and nothing to show when it's over but a memory you don't want of a time that didn't mean anything. With you—"

Out on the dark pond, one of the loons hooed softly. From somewhere away on the water, its mate answered.

"With you feels like being here. This is the only place I've ever really been safe." She looked up, and Kare saw the plea in her eyes, the prayer that the sanctuary of this place not be compromised, for if all else had failed her, this was what Elen would have: this porch, this pond, these loons haunting the night with their songs; these were the things that gave her depth and serenity, a sense of inner calm so profound it made her ache in that desperate, helpless way love makes one ache, a pain of growth and substance.

She offered her hand and pulled Elen gently to her feet.

"Kare, I'm so scared. If I can't—"

"Let me just hold you," Kare said softly. "Hurt can happen all at once, honey, but healing never does. We've got time."

Kare brushed her teeth; Elen banked the fire. Elen brushed; Kare, taller, closed the cocks of gas lamps mounted

by men of a long-legged clan. In the bedroom, she touched a
match to the wick of a kerosene lamp, and trimmed the wick
down low, golden light on golden logs, and turned to see Elen:
slight, almost fragile in a thin T-shirt and old fatigue pants,
watching her as if she were an eagle and Elen an osprey with
a fish. "I won't hurt you," she said softly, almost a reflex to
that wariness.

A smile—or something like one—flickered across that
shadowed face before Elen half-turned, not away from her
but in small modesty, to slip out of her shirt; she dropped it
to the chest beside the bed and reached for the buttons of her
pants. Her hands hesitated there, and it seemed forever to Kare
before those slender arms crossed over small, taut breasts to
hold herself by the shoulders, and longer still before the
whisper came: "Kare, help me. Please."

She was still cool from the pond, shy as a dog kicked
too often when Kare took her into her arms; she held her,
waited with her. At last the trembling stopped and Elen sighed
shakily into her throat, her hands finding Kare's waist. "I'm
sorry—"

"There's nothing to apologize for, Elen. We've got
time."

The laugh shivered from her. "Only five weeks." But
she lifted her face, brushing a tentative kiss against Kare's
jaw, and because she knew she must, Kare took delicate
control. She took Elen's face in her hands, finding her lips
with her own, and knew she had never been so gentle as she
was with that kiss, her fingertips tasting Elen's throat, her
face, her hair, until she felt Elen relent, accepting her touch;
Kare felt the subtle shift in them both as she found Elen's
tongue with her own. She only knew one way to make love,
and that was to let every feeling, every emotion, every sensa-
tion have its way with her, whether she gave or received;

when Elen had touched her in their loving she had known how Elen's palms felt, filled with her own skin; now, her fingertips stroking slowly from Elen's shoulders to her waist, she was vibrantly aware of every fiber of the being she touched, and of her own, so that when the fit of their bodies changed, a shift so subtle it was sensed more than felt, she knew Elen had given something up, some thread of that rein she held so desperately. *God, Elen, how I love you.*

She didn't say it. She gave it through her touch, through the brush of her still-clothed breasts against Elen's smooth nudity, through her tongue as it was allowed entry into her lover's mouth; there was a tiny catch of breath as Elen's fingers found her throat inside the gentle discipline of her embrace. "Kare—"

She touched her cheek to Elen's, a bare brush of that fine golden hair that glowed in just-right sunlight on both their faces. "Am I going too fast?"

"You're making my legs weak," Elen whispered. "How can you be so gentle?"

"Because you let me." Her nails were long, strong, perfectly tapered; they were tools and weapons and now, she traced them up Elen's back so lightly she felt only the vibration of that bare, supple skin through them, and she felt the press of thighs against hers and knew another thread had broken.

"What are you doing to me?" It was barely a breath, a bewilderment, almost a prayer. "Kare—"

She drew Elen's lower lip between her own and smoothed her palms, open-fingered, across the tautly-mus-cled span of her shoulders and down her sides, drawing fingernails back up almost hard enough to leave tracks, and tasted the inside of Elen's lip with the bottom of her tongue and Elen's knees buckled under her; "oh my god," she moaned, her arms going around Kare's neck for the support of her as she fought to get her legs back, and Kare held her up and probed the tip of her tongue into the corners of Elen's mouth, feeling those old reins disintegrating as Elen gasped for breath. "Kare, I can't oh god I can't even stand up Kare please—"

The bed welcomed them, but something tightened in Elen once they were there; Kare felt that, and held her, her hands stilled against her, only her breath brushing lips that had been willing just moments ago, and when at last she laid her palm against Elen's belly she felt the bare, quivering song of fear in those telling muscles and she drew her close, a comfort and caring that might, at that moment, have come more from a mother than a lover. "It's all right," she said softly. "It's okay, Elen."

"I know you won't hurt me," Elen almost wept. "Why can't I let go?"

"Because it isn't time. It will be. It doesn't have to be tonight, baby. Don't force it. Just let me hold you, honey."

She hadn't known she could be so patient. When Elen sighed a shivering sigh and pressed her lips against Kare's throat, she started over; when the whisper came, "Please, I want to feel your skin against me," she slipped out of her clothes and came back to find Elen naked, too—but that telltale trembling was there under her hand when she laid a quiet, searching palm against Elen's belly. "I'm sorry—"

"Shhh. Let me hold you—" and she let Elen get used to the feel of their skins together before she touched her lips to the fragility of her collarbone, and her throat, and found her lips again, applying her own gentle reins when Elen might have assumed control; "Let me," she whispered. "Let me love you."

"I know you do. I know—"

Feel it, Elen. Feel it.

Kare let her body say it as the loons quivered their songs
on the night; she touched Elen with her hands, with her lips;
with her nose, the gentle way a cat will tell you she cares for
you; she touched her with her self.

She sought Elen's breast with her lips, her patience
strong but her need deepening past it as she felt the pulse of
their hearts. She traced one long-nailed finger in a feathery
caress across the rise of Elen's hip, and felt the catch of breath
that so many times had meant the no was coming; it didn't.
She let the tip of her tongue wander between Elen's breasts,
and drew damp circles around one nipple and then the other
as she smoothed her palm down the ripple of her ribs and the
hollow of her belly, loving the sculpture of her. She traced
each rib with her tongue, and felt Elen's fingers touch her
hair, not to stop her or lead her but just to touch her; delicately,
she flickered the tip of her tongue into Elen's navel, and felt
those fingers tighten in her hair, and heard the breath of her
whisper: "Kare, please—"

She let her lips touch that soft froth of pale, fragrant hair.
Ask for me, Elen. Ask for me. I can't until you do.

"Kare—"

Barely, she tracked her nails up the tender inside of
Elen's thigh. *Say it. Break the reins, Elen, say it.*

And she felt it ripple through the supple body under her,
a swelling of the breast, a hollowing of the belly, a rising of
the hips before the words came "Oh god oh Goddess please
I need you I want you ogod Kare yes—" and she took her first
taste of the only woman she had ever known would be in her
heart until she died, and when at last Elen's breath came
tearing short from her and her fingers locked in her hair and
a cry like pain and triumph escaped her *ogod Kare yes god
Kare yes please Kare now—oh, god, now—* she understood

how all those nights, all those times, Elen had been honest
when she said I'm okay; of all the orgasms this woman had
given her, there had been none like this one of feeling her
against her mouth, under her hands, in her scent and her taste
and her being, utterly given to her the way she had always
given herself so completely, so lost in the giving she could
only, finally, say her name. And when Elen drew her up to
fill her arms with her, to tremble against her, to whisper, "oh,
god, thank you," she couldn't protest even though she thought
she should; she could only whisper back, "I love you. Elen, I
love you—"

"I know." It was an affirmation, a joy, a triumph. "I
know. God, Kare, I know."

CHAPTER TWENTY

"How's that bird feel, Colonel? Sinkin' them ol' claws in yo' shoulder?"

Kare gave the sergeant in the mail room a smile. She didn't really know how the brand-new eagles on her shoulder felt; she only knew that when General Buckman had pinned them to her epaulets and offered his handshake and grinned, "You'll outrank me someday, Kare," he had been wrong. The last twenty months had been too long and too lonely, with too much time to consider too many questions; she knew it would only be a week, or perhaps ten days, before she informed him of her decision to retire. She was profoundly grateful that fate had put her back into Bill Buckman's immediate command; she knew he wouldn't ask questions she didn't want to answer.

Smiles for well-wishing students and colleagues had come harder as the day wore on, for it felt like a lie to accept their congratulations and predictions of how long it might be before the eagle was replaced by a star, but the smile she gave Ray Washington now was honest, for she liked him and knew he genuinely liked her; she let him see her weariness. "Yesterday you called me colonel, Ray. Today you call me colonel. Same shit, different day. That's how it feels."

"Diffe'nce be in yo' pocketbook come end of the month." He handed her a stack of envelopes. "Hold up, ma'am; you got a package, too."

She accepted the box, her spirits reviving at the return address: Squirt, 116 Dartmouth PQIME. *Thank you, Elen; I needed you today and here you are.*

"You so damn pretty when you smile at that ol' Squirt." Kare looked up, almost startled by the boldness of the compliment, but Sergeant Washington's eyes said only that he knew it had been a long day for her, and that Squirt was far away and sorely missed.

"You always lookin' fine, Colonel Woman. You see that ol' Squirt, you get beautiful." He'd been handing over her mail for almost two years, and had seen a lot of boxes with 'Squirt' in the upper left corner draw that smile from her as they crossed the counter. "Don't know how the fool stay away from you like he do. Was you my woman, I be right up next to you all the damn time."

"You're bold as brass today, aren't you," she smiled. "Sort your mail, Ray. I'll give Squirt your regards."

"Mmmmm-mmmm-mercy. Ain't that fine," he murmured as she walked away, and she couldn't help the smile; Ray was shameless—and fastidiously selective— with his flirtations.

"He's prime today," she warned Major Bernadette O'Reilly, whom Ray considered Colonel Dillinger's nearest competition in the awesome Caucasian-officer-field-grade category. "Watch your rear, or he will."

"Lay-dees! Oh my heart, you both together! It's the big one, Elizabeth!"

"Raymond, get a life!" she heard as she pushed open the door to thick June heat, and knew Ray and 'Dette would be ten minutes trading insults. She trotted down the steps and made eight minutes of the usually ten-minute walk to her quarters, itching to see what Elen had sent; these little brown-paper-wrapped packages always held a new treasure to cherish.

First had come the osprey feather in a shadow box over a photograph of the pond; two weeks later there was a breathtaking statuette of an ancient Greek woman, with a hardback edition of the writings of Sappho. A month later came an exquisitely-carved wooden loon. Then a gold claddagh necklace with a heart-shaped ruby; she'd had it appraised for insurance and had almost fainted to hear what it was worth. She wore it all the time, even in the shower.

On Valentine's Day a dozen roses had been delivered to her office in the morning, a dozen in the afternoon to the classroom where she taught military strategy, another dozen that evening to her quarters. In her kitchen window was a faceted crystal that sent shimmering rainbows everywhere when the sun struck it; in the living room was the enlarged photo of her and Ezra grinning over a two-pound trout. By her bed was a photograph of the cabin in winter, almost buried in snow; they had spent three weeks of Christmas in that frozen, loonless quietude, and leaving had been wrenchingly hard for her.

One April day she'd gotten home to find Elen lounging on her front steps, spring-breaking in Kansas. A week after she left came a cassette with a Post-it note that said, "They're back," and she listened to ninety minutes of nothing but the voices of the loons; she listened to it almost every day.

The day after Elen had left, Bill Buckman had appeared at her office door. They spent a leisurely evening at the Officers' Club, ending up at her quarters for a late Drambouie; he told her his wife had left him. She'd heard that, she said; she was sorry. He allowed as to how he wasn't, particularly,

and asked her if she ever heard from Elen. "We're still very
good friends," she said, and he gave her the smallest of smiles;
she knew that if her answer had been different, he would have
asked her to dinner again the next evening. Instead, he told
her about the photograph on his office wall. "You looked
good together then," he said, and finished his drink and kissed
her cheek and left, and every Wednesday they had lunch and
talked shop and old times.

    Elen sent things: books and tapes and photos, and cards
that made Kare cry from laughter or aching missing her; she
sent flowers and cookies and once a box of fudge studded
with tiny sweet triangular nuts that the Post-it said were
beechnuts, and Kare wrote asking about beechnuts and got
back a six-page letter describing a day of bird hunting Elen
and Ezra had enjoyed, the pages so rich with detail Kare could
smell the woods and feel her feet cold in the October morning
and know her shoulder sore from a good day's work with the
shotgun; she could almost taste the partridge. "It tastes like
chicken cooked in cast iron on a green-pine fire scattered with
the seeds of a poplar tree," Elen wrote. "It tastes like a
delft-blue harvest sky with snow on the way, or like sunset
reflected on the water when the air is as sweet as the sweat
on your skin after making love. It tastes like the call of a loon,
and how it feels in the back of your heart to hear that with the
smell of the cookstove in the cool of evening; it tastes like the
sound of a paddle in early-morning water when the mist is
still thick on the pond, or like the sound of the river at night
when clouds half-cover the moon. It tastes like October."

    In that letter was a perfect orange maple leaf and a
grey-barred partridge feather—and for almost two years, that
was the only letter she had gotten from Elen. There were
Post-it notes, a few lines on greeting cards, a handful of brief,
loving poems, a trove of treasures that arrived in small boxes,

and a long phone call every Sunday, but there were no letters save the one.

But still, today she flipped through the envelopes first, seeing bills and offers for magazines and requests for donations. She sorted out the bills and sent most of the rest of it into the round file and made a drink from a bottle of thirty-year-old scotch Elen had sent; she poured from it only when there was a box to open. It was exquisite, and getting low; the Class VI store on post didn't stock it. She sipped and opened a tiny Victorinox knife ("you never know when you might need to rescue another hummingbird," the Post-it had said; she still hadn't figured that one out, and Elen had only smiled when she asked, but she carried the knife like she wore the claddagh) and cut the tape on the box.

"Open me first," said a Post-it on a silver-wrapped box that fit comfortably in the palm of her hand. She sat at the kitchen table of her apartment and used the knife to slit the tape on one end, drawing out a plush blue box that looked as if a jewelry store had been in its origins. "My god, child, you act as if you had money," she murmured, and lifted the lid.

And gasped. "My god—"

Three of them, perfect and sterling and not the eagles of a full colonel she had accepted this morning, although at first glance they might seem to be—

But eagles had a straight leading edge on the wing.

"Oh, Elen, my god—"

Ospreys had elbows.

The ubiquitous Post-it: "Congratulations, Goddess. Wear them if you dare."

Take their eagle, Kare. The osprey wins one when you do.

She didn't know how long she sat there, the blue velvet box held tight in her left hand close over her heart, her right hand over her eyes as she cried; she wasn't sure why she cried, except that something hollow and empty hit her so suddenly there was nothing else to do with the hurt but let it leak between her fingers.

She had never been married, but as she cried she knew divorce would feel like amputating a limb from her soul.

She had never left one lover for another, but she knew how that brutal duality of love and betrayal, of loss and gain, would feel.

She remembered her lover Rachel, and the nightmare of her death, and how long it had taken her to reconstruct her life around knowing she wouldn't be spending the rest of it with that wide-open laugh.

She remembered the first time she had heard the words 'fast track' applied to her own career. She had been a young captain when her brigade commander had taken a star from his own collar and put it in her hand and said, "You're on the fast track, Kare. You'll wear two or three of these before you're through." She remembered the smooth, sharp weight of that star between her fingers; she remembered how the hunger felt. That star was in a Dutch Masters cigar box in the cedar chest at the end of her bed—her hope chest, her last gift from her mother . . . before her mother had disowned her.

Briefly, with a sorrow so old and worn it barely remembered how to hurt, she remembered her mother.

She remembered looking in a mirror the day the general had given her that star and seeing elastic skin and lush auburn hair and defiant green eyes that challenged the world she had chosen *whenever you think you're man enough to derail me, come on. Come on.*

She remembered her mirror this morning: the tiny lines around her eyes, the flaring silver at her temples, the faintly-smiling assurance that said to those who might think to defy her or deny her. *You'll never be man enough, so don't even bother to try.*

She remembered Nikki Cole putting Craig Hogle on his knees, and shakily, she smiled. "Feisty little dyke," she whispered. "God, no wonder she loved you, Nikki. You were just me in a size small."

She remembered Sun Tzu: to win without fighting is best.

She looked at the chrome eagle on her cap, and at the silver ospreys in their lush blue box, and at the Post-it note stuck to the table.

Wear them if you dare.

With slow deliberation, she took the chrome-plated eagles from her cap and the epaulets of her jacket; she put the sterling silver ospreys in their stead. She picked the eagles from the table and rattled them loosely in her hand, a faint smile curving at a corner of her mouth as she looked at the osprey on her cap; one by one, she tossed the eagles across the kitchen to the wastebasket. They rattled in, metal against metal. "I dare," she said softly. "It's easy to dare when you don't have anything to lose."

"Unauthorized," the post commander would say four days later, standing too close to her so he could touch the osprey on her left shoulder, "but very handsome, Kare. Your stars will look just as good there." And she would smile, a smile as taut as barbed wire strung one high, thin note away from breaking, and the general would step away from her in uneasy confusion, some cautious, visceral thing in him shivering in deep warning, and over gin that evening he would think that if rattlesnakes could have green eyes, they would look like Colonel Kare Dillinger's eyes over that smile that was no smile at all

But now, 'open me first' meant there was something else; she tasted her drink and looked into the box, wondering what Elen could possibly do for an encore to three silver ospreys.

The second package was about the size of half a sheet of paper, not quite an inch thick. "Now I can write to you," said the Post-it; she puzzled briefly over it and stuck it on the table next to "wear them if you dare."

It felt like a paperback book, shy in its brown-paper wrapper after the plush blue box of the ospreys. There had been many books; their Sunday phone calls were often long and meticulous dissections of whatever novel Elen had sent last, and in the books and their discussion of them she had learned many things about herself and her lover. They filled the top shelf of a handsome little maple bookcase Elen had cautiously asked if she would like to have. "I made it for Nikki," she'd said. "She left it when she—she—she really liked you, Kare. I think she'd like for you to have it, but I'll understand if you—"

"You make damn sure you wrap it good when you send it to me," Kare had said softly. "I know what Nikki gave me." A few of the books in it—Twain's *Letters From The Earth*, Sarton's *Crucial Conversations*—said Nikki Cole in the front in smooth, slanted script.

She shook off the memory and cut the tape on one end of the brown paper, trying to guess: poetry, perhaps, to appease the deep emotion of the ospreys; maybe a biting satire, or some obscure opus of the previously unpublished works of F. Scott Fitzgerald, or—

"God, Elen! They say everybody's got a double," she murmured, seeing the author's photo on the back of the book when she slipped it face-down from the paper. "She looks enough like you to be—"

Photo by Kare Dillinger, said tiny print up the edge of the picture.

Her breath whooshed softly from her. "Elen . . .?" She turned the book over in her hands. "Oh, my god—"

Punchline.

She knew that shadowed mesa on the cover: it was Blackwell Mountain.

Elen McNally.

"You didn't tell me! Elen, you didn't tell me—" She turned it over again to meet those eyes: smoky, heavy-lidded, a smile that had always meant within the hour she would be gasping for breath; she recognized it then as one she had taken at the cabin towards the end of their Christmas stay there, using Elen's camera and asking for a print she had never gotten. Within an hour of that snap of the shutter they had both been naked and searching for breath; her belly fluttered with the memory of the taste of Elen on her tongue.

She opened the cover. There, in Elen's assertive printing:

"Kare, my Muse, my love. Linger a while: thou art so fair. Now: Elen"

And a deep and brooding red underlining smear; it could only be blood.

Colonel Kare Dillinger dissolved into helpless tears.

In Kansas City, thirty-five miles away, American Airlines Flight 1216 from Boston touched down. Elen McNally was on it.

About the Author

Nanci Little lives and writes on the coast of Maine.

 # Madwoman Press Titles

Lesbians in the Military Speak Out by Winni S. Webber
ISBN 0-9630822-3-X $9.95
Women from every branch of the armed forces tell their stories about being women and lesbians in the military.

Sinister Paradise by Becky Bohan
ISBN 0-9630822-2-1 $9.95
A professor of classics finds herself endangered by an international arms-smuggling conspiracy just as she finally finds love .

That's Ms. Bulldyke to You, Charlie! by Jane Caminos
ISBN 0-9630822-1-3 $8.95
Hilarious collection of single-panel cartoons that capture lesbian life in full. From dyke teenagers and lipstick lesbians, to the highly-assimilated and the politically correct.

On the Road Again by Elizabeth Dean
ISBN 0-9630822-0-5 $9.95
Magazine columnist Ramsey Sears tours America, finding adventure and romance along the way.

You can buy Madwoman Press books at your local women's bookstore or order them directly from the publisher. Send direct orders to Madwoman Press, Inc., P.O.Box 690, Northboro, MA 01532. Please include $2.50 for shipping and handling of the first book ordered and $.50 for each additional book. Massachusetts residents please add 5% sales tax. A free catalog is available upon request.